Gra

House

Jon Athan

For more information on this book or the author, please visit www.jon-athan.com. General inquiries are welcome.

Facebook:
https://www.facebook.com/AuthorJonAthan
Twitter: @Jonny_Athan
Email: info@jon-athan.com

Book cover by Sean Lowery: http://indieauthordesign.com/

Thank you for the support!

ISBN-13: 978-1986437820
ISBN-10: 1986437825

First Edition!

WARNING

This book contains scenes of intense violence and some disturbing themes. Some parts of this book may be considered violent, cruel, disturbing, or unusual. Certain implications may also trigger strong emotional responses. This book is *not* intended for those easily offended or appalled. Please enjoy at your own discretion.

Table of Contents

Chapter One

Don't Go to School Tomorrow

The text message read: *don't go to school tomorrow.* The message was followed by the emojis of a human skull above a pair of crossed bones and a handgun.

Marcus Ruiz, a high school junior, sat at the back of his classroom. He held his cell phone under the desk, hoping it wouldn't slip out of his clammy hands like a bar of soap in the shower. He stared down at the screen and read the message, then he read it again—and again, *and again.* He understood the meaning behind the message, it was a cliché threat, but he couldn't tell if it was genuine.

He glanced over at the back door of the classroom and thought: *he sent this yesterday, so something is going down today, right?*

He looked down at himself and cycled through the possibilities in his head. If a school shooter barged into the room, he figured he would be the first to go down. He was a scrawny, forgettable kid after all. He looked around the classroom and analyzed his classmates. *She would die, he would live, she would live, he would die,* he thought.

Marcus' eyes stopped at the classmate sitting at the desk beside him—Alex Munoz. Alex wasn't interested in the subject. He didn't enjoy reading books for his English class, so he fiddled with his cell phone under his desk instead.

Marcus leaned closer to Alex and whispered,

"Hey, did you get a text from Malcolm last night?"

Without taking his eyes off his phone, Alex nodded and responded, "Yup."

"So, um... What do you think?"

"About what?"

"About the text, man. You think he's serious?"

Marcus looked at the front of the classroom. Their teacher, John Crawford, sat at his desk and corrected essays while occasionally glancing over at his students. The students were supposed to be reading *The Great Gatsby* by F. Scott Fitzgerald. Most of the students read the novel while a few of them played with their phones. The white-haired teacher didn't notice anything out of the ordinary, though.

Marcus leaned even closer to Alex and asked, "Do you think he's going to come with a gun? I mean, um... do you know if his mom even owns any guns?"

"Nope."

"He probably bought one off of someone, huh? Caleb's dad has an AR-15 at home. I heard he's been trying to sell it for a while. What if Malcolm comes to school with that shit? What if–"

"He won't," Alex interrupted. He finally glanced over at Marcus. He whispered, "He's just fucking with us, man. It's just a meme, you know? 'Ha-ha, don't go to school tomorrow 'cause I'm going to shoot it up.' He wouldn't send something like that if he was actually going to do it. Don't worry about it."

Marcus reluctantly nodded in agreement. He stared at an empty desk next to the back door of the classroom—Malcolm's desk.

Malcolm was a sixteen-year-old high school junior. He was well known around school, but he often isolated himself. He wasn't interested in popularity. He stood five-eleven and had a sturdy physique. His hair was black and wavy, his eyes were brown and dark. The color of his eyes surprised some people because his mother had blue eyes. His father wasn't in the picture.

Marcus read the clock above the whiteboard: *9:25 AM.* He believed it was too early for a school shooting.

He tapped Alex's desk and asked, "Should we tell someone? What if he actually does it? Will we get in trouble?"

"I don't know, Marcus. I'm not a cop or a lawyer, man. If you're so scared, go tell on him. But, if it's a joke, you're just going to get him in more trouble. He'll probably get arrested for making threats or something."

"How do you know that? You said you weren't a cop."

"Just shut up already, man."

Marcus sighed and sank back into his seat. *We're all going to get in trouble because of him,* he thought, *shit, I should just ditch before lunch.* He opened his book and tried to read the chapter. After each page, he glanced over at the clock. Time moved at a snail's pace. One minute, two minutes, ten minutes, *twenty minutes*—a shooter didn't show up, gunshots didn't ring down the halls.

Barely negligible, Marcus murmured, "Fifteen more minutes... Come on, you stupid bell, just ring already. I want to–"

Mid-sentence, the back door burst open with a *crashing* sound. The door wobbled as it clashed with the door stop.

Malcolm entered the classroom. He wore a hooded sweatshirt, tight jeans, a beanie, and a bandana over his neck—black from head-to-toe. He didn't bother hiding his face, though. He wanted everyone to know *he* was responsible. His right hand was shoved into his hoodie pocket. The outline of a gun could be seen in his pocket.

He jumped on his desk and shouted, "Everyone get on the fucking ground! Get down!"

Most of the students glanced at each other and mumbled about the situation. They said different variations of the same thing: *is this some sort of joke? Is he pranking us?*

Marcus hit the floor like a man on fire, though, and Alex followed his lead. Other students, who also received the ominous text message, also hid under their desks. So, the skeptical students joined them and followed Malcolm's orders. The confused chatter in the classroom turned into frightened whimpers. They all shared the same thought: *I don't want to die.*

Crawford stood from his desk with his hands raised over his head. He said, "Malcolm, whatever you're–"

"Shut up," Malcolm barked. He lunged over to the desk in front of his. He said, "You're always talking, but you're never saying anything important. You're like the rest of the teachers at this damn school. You have no passion, no soul, *no heart.* You just read all of your lessons off of your textbooks, give us homework and tests, pass or fail us, then repeat. There is no 'connection' between us. You don't care about us. We're not friends, man."

He jumped over to the desk in front of him, then he lunged to the desk to his right. He watched as his classmates cowered under the desks.

He said, "None of us are friends, huh? We bully each other every day. I just saw some kid get bullied because he couldn't afford his lunch, because he couldn't eat. I mean, what kind of bullshit is that? What kind of school is this? He doesn't get lunch *and* he gets bullied. It's crazy, man!"

From under his desk, Marcus watched as Malcolm jumped from desk-to-desk until he reached the front of the classroom. He couldn't predict his next move. He knew Malcolm had a knack for pranks, but he also knew Malcolm was an angry person. He regularly argued with his teachers and fought with his classmates.

With his hand in his pocket, Malcolm wagged the gun at his teacher. He smiled and said, "You're an asshole. You've been trying to flunk me all semester, right? Why? Is it because I don't beg for help like the rest of these idiots? Is it because I won't suck your dick for better grades?"

In a soft tone, Crawford said, "I know you, Malcolm. You don't really want to do this. Whatever you have in your pocket—a knife, a gun, *whatever*—you don't want to use it. You don't want to hurt me or any of your classmates. You're a good kid. You've, um... You've made your point, though. Get down from there and let's talk about how we can make school a better place for all of us. Let's talk this out like men."

"Like men?" Malcolm repeated in an uncertain

tone. He crouched down on the desk, his hand still in his pocket. He jokingly asked, "Did you just assume my gender, Mr. Crawford?"

Some of the students snickered under their desks, tickled by the joke. The threat felt less severe thanks to Malcolm's sense of humor.

Crawford cracked a smile and said, "I knew this was a–"

"Shut up," Malcolm interrupted. "It was just a stupid joke. I didn't ask you to speak, I didn't let you run your mouth. We're playing by my rules now. *Mine,* not yours. Okay?"

Crawford nodded slowly, his hands trembling over his head. His eyes darted to the door to his right. He thought about running out of the room and calling for help, but he couldn't abandon his students.

Malcolm said, "Good. So, let's talk about this like 'men.' What makes a real man, Mr. Crawford? Hmm? Are you a real man? I mean, you fuck girls in exchange for good grades. You've had some of these girls gagging on your dick, haven't you? That's not how real men act, is it?"

Crawford shook his head and said, "That's not true at all. What are you talking about, young man?"

"I'm talking about your little 'extra credit' assignments. You're part of the problem, man. You abuse your power to molest these girls in exchange for good grades. You fuck them, Crawford!"

"That's not true."

"You're a child molester!"

"No, I am–"

"A child molester!"

Crawford said, "Repeating yourself over and over won't make it true, Malcolm. Now, please, get off the desk and take your hand out of your pocket slowly. Let's talk about what's really bothering you. Let's talk about–"

"Fuck you!" Malcolm shouted as he pulled his hand out of his pocket.

Crawford tightly closed his eyes and flinched, expecting a hail of bullets to penetrate his body. Instead, he heard the sound of a squeaky trigger. A squirt of water hit his face and dripped onto his button-up shirt. The teacher opened his eyes to a squint. He spotted the gun in Malcolm's hand—a plastic squirt gun.

The water gun was spray-painted black. From afar, it could have been mistaken for a real pistol. It had the shape of a handgun after all. From up close, it looked blatantly fake.

A devious grin on his face, Malcolm squirted him again and said, "Bang, bang."

A female student shouted, "Malcolm, you asshole!"

A jock said, "You're a dick, bro."

Marcus and Alex shared a sigh of relief, then they chuckled. Some of the other students weren't as forgiving. Some hurled books, pencils, and crumpled balls of paper at him. Others cried and ran out of the room, overwhelmed by the event.

Malcolm shrugged and asked, "What? Did I take it too far?"

Infuriated, Crawford grabbed Malcolm's arm and pulled him off the desk. The pair nearly tumbled to the floor in front of the whiteboard. Crawford dragged him out of the classroom. He muttered to himself as he headed to the principal's office.

Malcolm glanced back at the classroom and shouted, "I'm sorry, guys! It was just a prank!"

Chapter Two

Consequences

Malcolm leaned back in his seat, his arms crossed over his chest. Only the sound of his foot tapping emerged in the room. He didn't want to meet eyes with the principal, so he just stared at the desk in front of him. A landline phone, a picture frame, a pen bin, a computer monitor, a keyboard, and a manila folder sat on the desk. It was all neat and regular.

Eric Lawrence, the principal, sat on the chair opposite of him. Elbows on the table, he massaged his clean-shaved jaw and stared at the teenager. *Hmm*—the sound occasionally seeped past his sealed lips. His eyes were narrowed and his eyebrows were pulled in. He looked serious, angry, and disappointed. He ran his fingers across his bald head, leaned back in his seat, and sighed.

The pair waited in the small office. Lawrence had already scolded Malcolm and he had to wait in order to officially hand down his punishment, so there was really nothing else to say at the moment. After ten dreadful minutes, the door swung open. They simultaneously looked over at the door behind Malcolm and shared the same thought: *finally*.

Jennifer Hernandez, Malcolm's mother, stood in the doorway. The forty-year-old woman looked exhausted. She had black bags under her eyes and crows' feet on her cheeks. Her beach blonde hair was tied in a messy ponytail. She stood five-two with a thin figure, but she was strong and determined. She wore a blue collared shirt, black work pants, and work shoes.

As she walked into the office, Jennifer smiled at the principal and said, "I'm sorry I'm late. I was at work and I couldn't just leave, but I rushed over as soon as possible. It was–"

"It's okay, Ms. Hernandez," Lawrence interrupted. He beckoned to her and said, "Please take a seat."

As she sat down, Jennifer stared at her son and asked, "What did he do this time? I was told there was a–a... a 'commotion.' Is everyone okay? Is this... serious?"

Malcolm lowered his head and looked down at himself, trying to create a semblance of shame. In reality, he was only trying to stop himself from smiling and laughing. Lawrence leaned forward in his seat, his elbows on the desk and his fingers interlocked under his chin.

The principal said, "Well, Ms. Hernandez, your son ditched his first period class, then, when he finally decided to show up, he pulled another one of his infamous 'pranks' during second period."

Jennifer shook her head and blinked rapidly. She said, "Okay, um... I don't know how this could have happened. I dropped him off at school this morning. I watched him walk into this school with my own eyes, Mr. Lawrence."

"I understand, but he walked *off* before first period even started."

Jennifer stared down at her lap and, her voice burdened with shame, she asked, "So, what did he do?"

"He snuck back into school before 10:00 AM. He barged into his second period class and pretended to have a gun. He held his class hostage for several minutes, then he pretended to shoot his teacher. Fortunately, it wasn't a real firearm. He shot Mr. Crawford with a water gun that was painted black. But, as you can imagine, he terrorized his classmates and his teacher. He placed himself in danger, too. If a campus cop saw him, this could have ended very differently."

Terrorized—Malcolm huffed and shook his head upon hearing the word. He understood he broke the rules, he was willing to accept his punishment for that, but he thought the principal's statement was exaggerated. Terrorists *terrorized* people, teenagers just scared them. He couldn't help but snicker.

Teary-eyed, Jennifer glared at Malcolm and sternly said, "Do *not* laugh. This is not funny, young man. This is... Oh, God, how could you do this?" She placed her palm on her forehead and whimpered. She said, "I'm sorry, Mr. Lawrence. I'm so sorry. I've been trying my best to raise him right, I taught him better than this, but it's hard to raise a kid as a single mother. I can't be around all the time and I can't catch these sort of things when I'm always thinking about our next bill. I'm sorry, I'm not trying to make excuses. It's just... It's hard."

Lawrence said, "I understand that, Ms. Hernandez. Believe me, I get it. We've done our best to accommodate your situation. We've welcomed Malcolm into our free lunch program, we've given him opportunities to join our after-school clubs, and we've even offered extended counseling. We are as responsible for his actions as you, so I don't want you to blame yourself. However, we can't allow Malcolm's actions to go unpunished. This is a serious offense. A lot of kids are terrified right now. They are horrified, shaken, and... and disturbed. These kids are going to need counseling and their parents are going to want answers... and punishments."

Malcolm glanced over at the wall to his left. He ignored the certificates and awards on the wall. He had spent plenty of time in the principal's office before, so he knew the counselors' offices were right next door. He thought: *did I really scare them or are they just faking it?* At that moment, he was sorry for his actions.

Jennifer asked, "What kind of punishment are we talking about here?"

Lawrence responded, "Effective immediately, Malcolm will be suspended for fourteen days while the board, the parents, and the police discuss the matter. He may be expelled afterward and he may be charged with a possible felony. Ultimately, the severity of his punishment will depend on the reaction of the other parents and the police." He looked at Malcolm and said, "Ms. Hernandez, I think it would be best if you kept Malcolm out of trouble until we get everything under control. You can't make amends with people who decide his fate if he's out there terrorizing the community."

"I... I understand. I'll do everything in my power to make this right. We don't have a lot of money, but... I'll apologize. I'll grovel if I have to."

Malcolm scrunched his face and glanced at his

mother. His expression said: *jeez, mom, take it easy.* He looked back at the principal and clenched his jaw. *You're just making this worse, moron,* he thought, *stop exaggerating and let us go.* He was a troublemaker, but he knew how to pick his battles. So, he decided to stay quiet. He didn't want to aggravate the situation.

Lawrence said, "Listen, I know your situation is... *rough,* for lack of a better word. I think we all know Malcolm is a good kid at heart, too, despite some of his poor decisions. You won't need to grovel, but some heartfelt apologies can go a long way. Talk to the parents, let them know your situation. Both of you can get through this."

"Thank you, Mr. Lawrence," Jennifer said. She glared at Malcolm and asked, "Do you have anything to say?"

Malcolm stared at his principal, then at his mother, then back at his principal. He coughed to clear his throat and he leaned forward in his seat.

He said, "Um... I'm sorry for scaring my classmates. Some of them are actually my friends so, you know, I didn't want to hurt them. I hope they get through this." Lawrence smiled—a hopeful smile. Before the principal could say a word, Malcolm said, "I'm not sorry for making Crawford piss himself, though. He deserved that."

"*Malcolm,*" Jennifer snapped.

Lawrence sighed, then he said, "It's okay, it's alright. Just... try to keep him out of trouble. I'll call you when I have any updates. The police will be in contact with you soon, too. Probably in a few hours, actually. They've already had their chance to scold

Malcolm, but they won't be filing any criminal charges for a few days. You still have time to fix this. Okay?"

"I understand," Jennifer responded.

The adults stood from their seats and shook hands.

Jennifer said, "Thank you for everything, Mr. Lawrence. Again, I'm so sorry for all of the trouble."

"It's fine. Have a nice day."

Jennifer grabbed Malcolm's arm and gently pulled on his limb while glaring at him, as if to say: *don't make me drag you out.* Malcolm threw his backpack over his shoulder. He nodded and winked at his principal as he stood up. He followed his mother through the administration building.

He watched as his mother apologized to everyone in her path. She even apologized to the secretary on their way out. Malcolm thought: *overkill, mom, overkill.*

They hopped into an old black sedan in the parking lot. They sat in silence for a minute—a long, dreadful minute—while the rest of the students followed their regular schedules in the school. Malcolm stared at his mother, waiting for her to speak. He wanted her to scream, he even thought a slap to the face would be appropriate, but she just stared at the steering wheel. The silence was deafening.

Malcolm said, "I'm sorry. It was just a stupid prank, mom. I didn't think it would go this far. I thought I'd get detention for a few weeks or suspended for a few days. I didn't want this to happen."

"You could get expelled, you could go to juvie," Jennifer said, her eyes glued to the steering wheel.

"I know. I really am sorry, mom."

"Yeah, I'm sorry, too. Now I have to spend the next two weeks fixing this. Christ, what am I going to do with you?"

"I don't know. Just scream or ground me or... or hit me. Just do something already. I hate feeling like this. I hate feeling guilty. It sucks. Come on, get mad at me. Do something."

Jennifer's eyes widened as an idea struck her. She looked simultaneously optimistic and afraid. Her eyes became dim while her mouth twisted into a smile. She reversed out of the parking space and started navigating the parking lot.

Baffled, Malcolm asked, "Mom, what's up with you?"

Without looking at her son, Jennifer said, "I have an idea to... to keep you out of trouble. Let's go home and get you packed. It's time for you to meet your grandfather."

Chapter Three

The Arrival

The black sedan rolled to a stop in front of a white two-story house. Jennifer sat in the driver's seat, Malcolm sat in the passenger's seat. A duffel bag, the size of the largest carry-on bag, sat in the backseat. Jennifer appeared antsy, like a cheating spouse on the verge of being caught. Malcolm, on the other hand, looked confused but curious. The pair had spent ninety minutes traveling from Los Angeles to some cozy neighborhood in a no-name city in Southern California.

At first sight, the differences were jarring. The neighborhood was eerily tranquil. It resembled something from the good old days—white picket fences, clean sidewalks, and freshly clipped hedges and mowed lawns. Some housewives worked on their gardens while some elders swung on their porch swings. A few kids played tag on the street, yapping and screaming—the school day had already ended for the younger children. The residents all seemed respectful to each other.

The quietude of the neighborhood gave off an eerie vibe—*an alien feeling.*

Malcolm thought: *holy shit, this place is crazy, these can't be real people.* It wouldn't surprise him if the residents left their doors unlocked throughout the night. And, if that were the case, he figured it would be easy to burglarize them.

As he ran his eyes over the white house, he said, "So, we drove an hour and a half... *for this?*"

Jennifer stared at the dashboard and said, "Yes."

"Why?"

Jennifer didn't tell Malcolm much about their trip prior to departing. She only gave him the short version: *pack a bag, you're going to meet your grandfather.* She finally turned in her seat and looked at her son. She tried to smile, but the side of her mouth twitched uncontrollably. Her eyes were dry, but she looked as if she could burst into tears at any moment.

She said, "You're going to be staying with your grandparents for a few days, maybe even a few weeks. I need you to stay out of trouble while I'm taking care of things back home. I'm going to be... I guess I'm going to be begging for some, um, leniency. I'm going to do my best to save you, sweetie."

"What is staying with some old people going to do?"

"Hey, they're not just 'old people.' They're your grandparents. Respect your elders, Malcolm," Jennifer said. "Listen, my dad is old, you're right about that, but he's also tough. You've never met anyone like him. You may think some of your teachers were hard-asses, but... but you haven't seen anything yet. He'll teach you a thing or two about respect."

She looked over at the house, her eyes dilated with fear. Although she wasn't quite panicking, her breathing intensified and her body trembled. A mere glimpse of the house caused a downpour of forgotten memories to flood her mind. She glanced back at her son, trying her best to keep her composure.

In a soft, awed voice, she said, "He broke me when I was younger and, honestly, I was probably worse than you. I used to sneak out at night to smoke and drink and party and... and he'd always be waiting for me when I got back. It was impossible to get anything past him. I didn't like his methods, but I appreciated him, you know? He was only doing what he thought was the right thing to do. I get that now."

Malcolm smirked and said, "Wow, mom, it sounds like you were a real badass. Now we know where I get it from, huh? I wonder if dad gave me some of his 'bad' genes, too."

The interior of the vehicle became silent. The sounds of joy—kids chatting and playing—barely seeped into the car, muffled and faint.

Jennifer said, "Speaking of your father... There's something you should know before you meet your grandparents. I loved your father, but my dad never liked him. He technically disowned me because I married your dad."

"Damn, what did dad do to him?"

"He didn't do anything. It was just his... his existence that made my father angry. It's hard to say it, but, well, your grandfather doesn't like Mexicans or... or anyone who even looks Hispanic. I guess he just doesn't like other races very much."

Malcolm opened his mouth to speak, but he couldn't say a word. The revelation struck him like a bolt of lightning. He looked over at the house, then back at his mother.

He asked, "Are... Are you kidding me? He knows he lives in Southern California, right? There are Mexicans everywhere."

"I know, I know. Listen, your grandfather doesn't *hate* other races, he just didn't want us to, you know... *blend.* He wanted me to stay 'pure' or whatever. He's not the type to burn a cross on his lawn or dress as a ghost in the woods or anything like that. He doesn't walk around the streets yelling slurs or discriminating against people. He's just from a different generation. Don't take it personally."

"Don't take it personally? You know I'm half-Mexican, right?"

"Of course I do. I'm your mother, kiddo."

"Yeah, so this guy probably hates me already. And you're just going to leave me here? Really?"

Jennifer sighed, then she said, "It's going to be fine. He might make some ignorant remarks, but he won't hate you. Like I said, he's just from a different generation. He was raised with a different mindset. That doesn't excuse his actions, but it explains 'em."

Malcolm muttered, "Great. They're old *and* racist. This is going to be one shitty vacation."

Once again, silence dominated the interior of the car. The sounds from the street were smothered. Jennifer caressed Malcolm's hair as she stared at him. Malcolm loved his mother, he didn't mind her gesture of affection, but he felt uncomfortable in the car. To him, it felt as if they were saying their final goodbyes.

Malcolm asked, "What? Why are you looking at me like that?"

Jennifer smiled and said, "It's nothing. I just... I

love you so much, sweetheart."

"*O*–kay... I love you too, mom."

Jennifer patted Malcolm's shoulder and said, "Go ahead. Grab your bag and get in there."

For a second, Malcolm thought about begging his mother to let him stay at home. *No,* he thought, *I've caused enough trouble for her, I'm not a little kid.* He leaned back and grabbed his bag. He opened the door, then he stopped. He noticed his mother was still seated, strapped to her seat with one hand on the steering wheel.

He asked, "Aren't you going to walk me in? I mean, how do you know they're even here?"

Jennifer said, "They're home. My dad disowned me, I haven't spoken to him in decades, but I stayed in contact with my mother. She even sent us some money a few times. I made all of our arrangements with her last night. This is their address. This is the time we agreed on. They know you're coming and they're expecting you. Go on, get in there. Don't keep them waiting."

"Okay. I guess this is goodbye, then."

"Goodbye, Malcolm. I'll see you soon, baby," Jennifer said. As Malcolm climbed out of the car and closed the door, she shouted, "Behave yourself, sweetie!"

Malcolm stood in front of the picket fence and stared at the house. The house was quiet and nice, but it still managed to frighten him. He pushed the gate open and strolled up the walkway, counting each slow step. Before he knew it, he found himself on the porch, standing in front of a burgundy door. He glanced back at the street—his mother still watched him.

He took a deep breath, then he rang the door bell. The sound of wheels howling echoed through the street as his mother peeled out of her parking space and sped away.

Malcolm looked back and muttered, "Gee, mom, thanks for nothing."

Chapter Four

We're Family, Not Friends

After a minute, the front door swung open. Barbara O'Donnell, Malcolm's grandmother, stood in the doorway. At sixty-five years old, she stood four-eleven with a roly-poly figure—short and round. She wore a blue house-dress with a floral pattern and matching slippers. Her white hair was short and wavy. Her flabby cheeks inflated as she grinned.

The elderly woman said, "Oh, I haven't seen you around here before, young man. You must be Malcolm, right? Malcolm Hernandez?"

Malcolm smiled, nodded, and said, "Yeah."

"Oh, I knew it! I felt your presence before I even came to the door! I'm so happy to see you, my handsome little man!"

"I guess I'm happy to–"

Before he could finish, Barbara lunged forward and hugged him. She whispered something as she nuzzled his chest. Malcolm stood an entire foot taller than her, so he saw the top of her head when he stared down at her. He didn't know how to react to his grandmother's affectionate gesture. She stood on her tiptoes and kissed his cheek—an innocent peck.

Barbara held his hands and said, "I've always wanted to meet you, honey. My name is Barbara, but you can call me Grandma Babs. Oh, what am I saying? Your mother has probably told you everything about me, hasn't she?"

"To be honest, I didn't even know you existed until yesterday," Malcolm responded, a nervous smile on his face.

"Well, I've known about you since you were born. You look like such a sweet boy... Come in, come in."

Malcolm walked into the house, the duffel bag in his right hand. He examined his surroundings as his grandmother closed and locked the door. The front door opened up to the living room. There was a three-seat sofa, a recliner, a glass coffee table, and a flat-screen television to the right. Picture frames and bookshelves clung to the walls above the console tables and dressers. Shadows cloaked the spines of the books, but they appeared to be old novels.

The living room was seamlessly connected to the dining area, which resided to the left of the front door. The dining area had a rectangular dining table and a cupboard. On the parallel wall from the front door, from left to right, there was an archway, another door, and a staircase leading to the second floor. The archway led to the kitchen. The sound of a running faucet entered the living room through the archway.

Barbara patted Malcolm's ass and said, "Sit in the recliner, honey. It's one of the most comfortable seats in the house."

Malcolm furrowed his brow upon feeling his grandmother's hand on his bottom. She didn't hit him hard, she wasn't trying to hurt him, but the gentle spanking unnerved him. *Don't cause a scene, Malcolm,* he thought, *maybe she just likes you, maybe this is just how old people act.* Rosy-cheeked, he smiled at his grandmother—and his grandmother smirked in return.

The teenager sat in the recliner and placed the duffel bag on his lap. He watched his grandmother with a set of curious eyes.

Barbara stood behind the sofa and said, "Your grandfather is in the kitchen. He's washing the dishes like a gentleman. Don't worry, he'll be out soon. I think he'll be happy to see you, too."

Malcolm could only respond with a nod. He thought: *drop the act, grandma, I know you're married to a racist.*

Barbara continued, "I've seen you so many times in your birthday pictures. Your mom stopped sending them a few years ago, though. I don't know why."

Malcolm fiddled with his cell phone and said, "It's probably because I stopped having birthday parties three years ago, so she stopped taking birthday pictures."

"Oh, that's too bad. I felt like I lost you when I stopped getting those pictures. We should all celebrate your next birthday as a family. How does that sound, honey?"

If I'm not in juvie—Malcolm stopped himself from uttering the response. Instead, he responded with a noncommittal shrug. The sound of the running faucet came to an abrupt stop. The sound of boots *thudding* on linoleum tiles immediately followed. Malcolm and Barbara glanced over at the kitchen archway.

Ronald O'Donnell, Malcolm's grandfather, stood in the archway, drying his hands with a small white towel. His piercing blue eyes were stuck on his grandson—and Malcolm stared back at him.

Ronald was sixty-eight years old, he stood five-eight, and he wore a white t-shirt, navy Dickies work pants, and a pair of steel-toe boots. He looked stern and angry, a perpetual scowl plastered on his wrinkled face. His white hair was slicked back with goops of gel. He had a goatee, too, white and trimmed.

Malcolm thought: *he's going to be a tough son of a bitch, isn't he?*

Ronald threw the towel over his shoulder and walked into the living room. He muttered, "You boys are always late, aren't you? You never change, lazy bastards..." He stopped beside his wife and coughed to clear his throat. In a loud, clear voice, he said, "My name is Ronald O'Donnell. You can address me as sir, grandfather, or Mr. O'Donnell. We are not on first-name basis. We're family, not friends. You don't have to like me and I don't have to like you. Understood?"

Malcolm said, "Yes, sir."

"Good. Now, put your phone in your bag and give us your full attention, son."

Malcolm raised his brow and cocked his head back, as if to say: *excuse me, are you serious?* He glanced over at his grandmother. To his utter surprise, she just smiled and nodded at him. He sighed and shoved his phone into the duffel bag. For his mother's sake, he wanted to start his relationship with his grandparents on the right foot.

Ronald said, "Good. Now we can get down to business. First and foremost, welcome to our home. We would greatly appreciate it if you didn't steal anything during your stay. I know your people have a knack for that, but it won't do you no good if you steal from us. Take that as your first and final warning."

Malcolm chewed on his bottom lip and glared at his grandfather, fighting the urge to argue with him. His father vanished when he was young so he wasn't familiar with his Chicano roots, but he was still insulted by his grandfather's shameless racism. *Go fuck yourself, old man,* he thought.

Ronald said, "You may not know us, but we know you. You are here because your mother asked for our assistance. No, she *begged* for our assistance. Your mother and I aren't on good terms, but she's family—and family takes care of family. It's been a while since I've done her a favor anyway. I–"

"Decades, right?" Malcolm said.

"Don't interrupt me, boy," Ronald snapped.

Malcolm sucked his lips inward and leaned back in his seat, surprised by his grandfather's hostility. *Damn, he really hates me,* he thought, *so much for getting on his good side.* He decided to bite his tongue in order to avoid his grandfather's wrath.

Ronald said, "As I was saying: I feel like I owe your mother a favor. And you caught my attention, boy. She told us about your 'behavioral issues.' She told us about the fighting, the ditching, the pranking... She told us everything. You might be a problem for your mother and your deadbeat father, that damn coward, but you won't be a problem for me. No, boy, I'm going to fix you. I'm going to save you from those bad genes you inherited."

Ronald and Malcolm quietly stared at each other.

Ronald looked cold and angry, waiting to snap at Malcolm at the first sign of defiance. Malcolm wanted to say something—*anything*—but he didn't know if it was his turn to talk. Barbara still grinned and nodded, unreasonably happy like a peppy life coach.

Barbara tapped Ronald's arm and said, "The rules, honey. You need to tell him the rules."

"Right, right."

Ronald slowly walked around the sofa, his eyes glued to his grandson. He stopped next to the recliner and towered over Malcolm. Malcolm stared up at him, but he didn't say a word. He thought: *is this old ass clown really trying to intimidate me right now?*

Ronald said, "We cooked up some rules for you, boy. They're very simple and very reasonable, but I'm sure you'll manage to break them somehow. Your kind always does." He snorted and coughed to clear the mucus from his throat, then he said, "First, you must always ask for permission to leave this house. You are allowed on the front porch and the backyard, but you're not allowed to leave this property without our permission. Understood?"

"Yes, sir."

"Secondly, if your friends manage to find you here or if you somehow manage to make friends in our wholesome little city, you must ask for permission before you invite them to our house. I will not allow this home to be invaded by a bunch of taco-heads. We already have you here and I don't want to deal with a damn infestation. You got that?"

You're an asshole and you deserve to be shot—the

words were clogged in Malcolm's throat. He clenched his fists, gritted his teeth, and nodded.

Ronald continued, "You won't be going out often, but you will still have a curfew. You better be in this house by 1700. That's 5:00 PM, boy. While you're at home, you will be given three meals: breakfast, lunch, and dinner. Babs will be in charge of your diet. You eat what she serves you and nothing else. If you're still hungry, ask Babs before pillaging the fridge. Your father was an animal, but you're not like him. Not now, at least."

Chiming in, Barbara softly said, "Don't forget about the attic and basement, Ronnie."

"Right," Ronald said as he looked over at his wife. He turned his attention to Malcolm and said, "Only three rooms will be off-limits during your stay: our bedroom, the attic, and the basement. You will only go into the basement and our bedroom to complete your chores. You will *never* go into the attic. Do you understand me, boy?"

Malcolm nodded in agreement. The rules were strict, but he expected worse from an old racist. He was concerned about the potential consequences for breaking the rules, though.

Ronald said, "I didn't ask you to nod, boy. Do you understand me?"

Malcolm responded, "Yeah."

"Yeah? That's not going to cut it. Do I need to give you a multiple-choice question? Huh? Do you need a list of acceptable answers? Are you that–"

"Yes, sir," Malcolm said, his voice louder than his grandfather's.

Ronald stared at his grandson, his face contorted

with anger, then he cracked a smile and nodded. His gesture said something along the lines of: *good boy, good boy.*

He said, "You're finally getting it. Just remember: don't interrupt me." He patted Malcolm's shoulder and said, "Put your bag on the ground and follow me to the basement."

"The basement?" Malcolm repeated in an uncertain tone.

"Yes, the basement. It's the first stop on our tour —and the most important stop, too."

Malcolm placed the bag on the ground beside the recliner. He followed his grandfather to the door between the kitchen archway and the staircase. Ronald opened the door, revealing a staircase leading down to the basement. He flicked a switch on the wall, washing the room with a white glow. The fluorescent lights were powerful.

Ronald said, "Let's go."

Malcolm stood in the basement doorway and watched as his grandfather walked down the stairs. Since the stairs weren't completely enclosed, he could see into the basement, too. From above, it looked like a normal basement. Still, he got an ominous vibe from the room. *Just like that Jack Ketchum book,* he thought, *I'm going to be the boy next door.*

He glanced back at his grandmother, who still stood next to the sofa. She smiled and nodded at him, as if to say: *go on, don't keep him waiting.*

Malcolm returned the smile, then he went down the stairs. The stairs groaned with each slow step, as if the stairs were crying—as if he could fall through them at any moment. He stopped at the bottom of the stairs and looked around.

At first glance, the basement looked normal. There was a workbench to the right, tools hanging on the wall above the table. On the left, there was a heater, a washing machine, and a drying machine. There were also some shelves, which stored canned goods and other non-perishables. Piles of cardboard boxes sat at the corners of the room, filled with old belongings and unintentionally decorated with cobwebs.

Malcolm's eyes were fixated on the wall on the other side of the room, though. There was a heavy iron door at the center of that wall. There was a viewing slot—*a peep door*—at the top of the door and a longer, thinner slot at the bottom of the door —*a tray slot.* It resembled the door of a prisoner's cell.

As his grandfather unlocked the door, turning a knob and moving the latches, Malcolm asked, "What's in there?"

Ronald pushed the door open. The mysterious room was impenetrably dark. The light from the main room in the basement barely illuminated the other room.

Ronald said, "Get in there. Take a peek."

Malcolm smiled nervously and said, "I... I don't think so."

"What? Don't tell me you're afraid of the dark, boy. Shit, I can rehabilitate you, but I can't save you from a boogeyman that doesn't exist."

"It's not that. I just... I don't want to go in there."

Ronald stared at Malcolm with a deadpan

expression. He huffed and shook his head. He was either amused or frustrated—or both. Outside of the room, he flicked a switch next to the door. A bulb dangling from the ceiling illuminated the mysterious room. However, unlike the bright fluorescent lighting in the main room of the basement, a mustard-yellow light lit up the room.

In a condescending tone, Ronald asked, "Bright enough for you, kid?"

Malcolm leaned to his left and gazed into the other room. To his utter surprise, the room appeared to be unfurnished. *No traps,* he thought, *it's just an empty room.*

As he approached the doorway, Malcolm asked, "Why do you want me to go in there? What's so special about this room?"

"It's supposed to be a bunker. It won't survive a nuke from that fat, gook-eyed bastard in North Korea, but it'll keep your grandmother safe from other national 'emergencies.' Something's coming in this country and we have to be ready."

"Only grandma? What about you?"

"Me? Shit, boy, if I'm not dead, I'm going to be on the frontlines, just like every other proud American who bleeds red, white, and blue."

Malcolm took his first step into the room and glanced around. It was a small, twelve-by-twelve-foot room. There wasn't a single piece of furniture in sight. The floor, the ceiling, and the walls were made of concrete. There were a few cracks and stains, but none of it seemed irregular.

As he glided his eyes over the walls, Malcolm asked, "Why are you showing me this?"

"I figured you'd want to see it. This could be your room, depending on your behavior. I always thought it would make a nice den or 'bachelor's pad.' That kind of thing."

Malcolm took another step forward. He leaned forward and peeked behind the door. For some odd reason, he expected a serial killer to be standing in the corner of the room. He searched for a reason for his visit to the bunker, even if it didn't make sense. *He's not trying to kill me,* he thought, *so what am I really doing here?*

Before he could confront his grandfather about it, the sound of squeaky hinges broke the silence in the bunker. Wide-eyed, he glanced over his shoulder and watched as the door closed behind him.

He shouted, "Hey! What the hell, man?!"

He rushed to the door. As he reached for the knob, *clinking* and *clanking* sounds emerged from the other side. He twisted and wiggled the knob, but to no avail—the door was locked. He struck the door with the bottom of his fists, he rammed it with his shoulder, and he kicked the tray slot.

He shouted, "Let me out, damn it! Stop fucking with me! I swear, I'm going to–"

The light went out and darkness filled the room —a cold, pitch-black darkness. A slit of light barely seeped into the room through the thin crack under the door.

His voice muffled because of the door between them, Ronald shouted, "Listen up, boy! You're going to be spending some time in there by your lonesome. That means: *minimal human contact.* You might get a meal, but you won't participate in any other form of communication. I need you to understand that I mean business. You hear me?"

Awed by the explanation, Malcolm muttered, "Holy shit, he's actually insane..."

Ronald continued, "Think of this as a non-physical punishment for your past actions. I know your naive mother hasn't punished you before. She would think this is 'wrong' or 'immoral,' but I know it's going to help you. If all goes well, you should be out of there in no time." As he approached the bottom of the stairs, he shouted, "In prison, they call this 'the hole!' Around here, we call it 'purgatory!' You'll atone for your sins here and you'll be born a new man! A *real* man!"

Upon hearing the creaky stairs—a very soft sound—Malcolm banged on the door and yelled, "Don't leave me here! You can't do this to me! You can't fuckin' do this to me! It's illegal!"

Legal or illegal, moral or immoral, none of it mattered to Ronald. The slit of light vanished in the bunker and the faint sound of a door slamming barely entered the room. The old man was gone.

Surrounded by darkness, Malcolm muttered, "What the fuck, man?"

Chapter Five

Purgatory

Malcolm looked up and shouted, "Alright, I get it! I've had enough of this time-out bullshit! Let me out of here!"

He held his breath and listened to the house. He didn't hear the creaky floorboards, the groaning pipes, or the outside world. The bunker was completely silent. His grandparents ignored him. He let out a long, loud exhale of frustration. He had trouble taming his anger.

He banged on the door and yelled, "Stop fucking with me, man! I didn't do anything to deserve this! I listened to you, I followed your rules. I thought you were a man of your word, but you're not. You're just a racist bitch!" He kicked the door and shouted, "Shit! Let me go, damn it!"

Malcolm took three steps back and stared forward. He could barely see the door through the darkness, but he knew it was in front of him. Yet again, there was no response. The thick concrete walls and the heavy door confined him to a puny bunker, trapping him in an abyss of nothingness. He felt like he was in a different world.

He whispered, "He's actually serious about this. The old man is crazier than I thought. What do I do now? What *can* I do now?"

His eyes widened as an idea dawned on him. He shoved his hands into his jean pockets, then he shoved them into the pockets of his navy windbreaker jacket.

"Where the hell is it?" he muttered as he patted his jeans and jacket. He stopped his search, grunting and groaning. He said, "Shit. I put my phone in my damn bag. He planned this from the beginning. Damn it, he's crazy and smart..."

He turned around and tried to examine the bunker, searching for a way out. He had hoped he missed something—*anything*—during his initial inspection of the room. His vision improved with each passing second, but he still couldn't see much. So, he touched the frigid wall on the left side of the door with his fingertips and walked beside the wall.

His fingertips glued to the walls, he walked from corner-to-corner until he reached the right side of the door. During his short walk, he noticed some holes on the ground that formed a seven-by-two-foot rectangle. The holes were puny, likely drilled with a hammer drill. He thought: *what are those for, grandpa?* There were more puny holes at the center of the room, but he could barely see them.

Other than the holes, he didn't notice anything of significance in the bunker. It was just an empty room.

He leaned back on the door and sighed. The total darkness blinded him. It was a jarring and horrifying sensation. It addled his mind and warped his perception of reality. His eyes were wide open, but he actually started to believe his eyes were closed. He placed his thumb and index fingers on his eyelids, ensuring his eyes stayed open.

"Damn it, I'm already going crazy," he muttered.

"How long has it been since he locked me in here? A minute? Two? Five? No, it's been longer. It's been... ten or fifteen minutes. Longer than that? I don't know anymore. What am I doing? Who am I even talking to?"

He turned around and faced the door. His hands hovered over the door as he slowly reached for it. He shuddered as soon as he felt the cold iron. His face was cloaked by the darkness, but his expression of relief said: *there you are!*

He knocked on the door and shouted, "Hey! I'm ready to come out! I'll, um... I'll behave myself, I promise! Grandma Babs, please let me out!" No one answered. He lowered his arms to his sides and said, "I don't want to be here anymore. Please let me out. Please..."

Solitude and boredom often had unpredictable effects on the human mind. In complete isolation, surrounded by nothing, most people would prefer *pain* to boredom. People would actually use trivial methods of self-harm as a form of entertainment because it would give them something to do. Solitude and boredom were forms of torture.

Out of sheer boredom, Malcolm closed his eyes and gently banged his head on the iron door—*tap, tap, tap.* The banging wouldn't cause any brain damage, but it certainly caused some pain to surge across the top of his brow. He couldn't stop himself, though. Despite the pain, he felt compelled to continue.

His rationale was simple: the literal head-banging would give him something to do and it would possibly send a signal to his grandparents.

His forehead planted on the door, Malcolm opened his eyes upon hearing a *clanking* sound. A slit of light entered the room through the crack under the door. The tray slot at the bottom of the door swung open and a plastic tray was pushed into the room. As the teenager fell to his knees, the tray slot was slammed shut.

Malcolm scratched at the slot and shouted, "Hey! Let me out! Please, don't leave me in here! I'm begging you! Grandma? Grandpa?"

The basement and the bunker remained quiet. He didn't hear any thudding footsteps or creaky stairs. He stared down at the plastic tray. Thanks to the slit of light, he could see the meal on the tray—a bowl of chicken soup and a cup of water. A plastic spork sat next to the bowl. As he examined the food, the slit of light vanished. His visitor was gone.

Malcolm hit the door and muttered, "Damn it..."

The teenager completely lost track of time, but he knew one thing for sure: he was hungry. So, he safely assumed it was past noon. He had spent at least ninety minutes in the bunker.

He whispered, "I might as well eat. This psycho might kill me if I don't. I can't starve, I can't let him win."

He dunked the spork into the soup, he fished out a chunk of chicken, then he slurped the soup off the spork. He grimaced in disgust. The broth was cold and sour while the chicken was stale and chewy. He finally caught a whiff of the soup's vile smell. The bowl emitted the pungent scent of rotten eggs.

He whispered, "What the fuck? Are they trying to poison me?"

Malcolm clenched his jaw and stared down at the bowl. He was disgusted by the food, but he feared he would starve if he didn't eat. He didn't know if he would get another meal during that day. So, he scarfed down three more pieces of chicken and a few chopped carrots, then he chugged the water. It was only eight measly ounces of water, but it helped him keep the food down.

He said, "That was sick. That was so sick. Why are they doing this to me? What the hell is going on here? What kind of house is this?" He looked over at the center of the bunker, disappointed. He said, "So... what do I do now?"

Malcolm had to relieve his boredom and kill time. So, he did whatever came to mind. He lay down on his back, then, like a child, he rolled on the floor. He rolled from wall-to-wall, back-and-forth. He remembered rolling on the ground with his classmates in preschool—maybe it was kindergarten. *Why was that fun?*–he thought. It certainly wasn't fun in the bunker. He stopped rolling after a few minutes.

He turned onto his stomach and started doing push-ups. One, two, three, four, five... *fifteen*—after the fifteenth push-up, he took a one-minute break. Then he fell back to the floor and did another fifteen. He repeated the process seven times, exercising until his arms gave out. To his utter disappointment, there were still no signs of his grandparents in the basement.

Again, Malcolm lay on his back. He would have been staring at the ceiling, but the darkness wouldn't allow him to see that far. So, he just closed his eyes and hummed. He tried to sing the catchy songs he heard on the radio like a human jukebox, but he couldn't remember all of the lyrics. He mumbled through the parts he didn't know.

His eyelids grew heavier with each passing second, but he couldn't fall asleep. The concrete floor caused his back and neck to ache.

He murmured, "I wanna go home... I wanna go home, man. I just want–"

Mid-sentence, the sound of *clinking* locks emerged in the room. The door swung open, causing a wave of light to pour into the bunker. Malcolm lifted his head from the floor and squinted at the doorway, his vision blurred by the light.

A dark figure stood in the doorway. The figure looked soft and wavy, as if he were seeing him through heat haze. After a few seconds, his vision adjusted and he finally recognized his grandfather in the doorway.

Scowling, Malcolm said, "You can't keep me down here forever. People will ask questions, people will look for me."

Ronald smirked and said, "I wasn't planning on keeping you down here, boy. I was only trying to teach you a lesson. You know the rules, we drew the lines, and now you know what happens when you misbehave."

"Are you kidding me? I could have died down here. I could have... I don't know, I could have tripped and smashed my head on one of these walls. I could have starved. I could have dehydrated, man!"

"We gave you food and water. You're grateful for that, aren't you?"

"It was rotten!"

"Watch your tone, boy," Ronald snapped. Malcolm clenched his jaw and cocked his head back. Ronald said, "You're acting like a spoiled brat—like a drama queen. Shit, boy, you were only down here for four, maybe five hours. Believe me, I've seen men go through a lot worse in my lifetime."

Malcolm was rendered speechless by the revelation. *Only five hours,* he thought, *it can't be possible, can it?* Five hours was the average time to travel from Oxnard, California to Las Vegas, Nevada in a car. It was a long but tolerable trip. In the bunker, however, five hours felt like five days. He was mentally and physically drained by the experience.

Ronald said, "At least you're still alive. That proves something to me."

"What?"

"It proves you're not a complete pussy like your deadbeat father. It proves you're a fighter and a survivor, like me. That's something to be proud of, son. Now, get your ass off that floor and follow me. I'll show you around before I take you to your real room."

From the floor, Malcolm watched as his grandfather walked away from the doorway and approached the stairs. The teenager was downright befuddled by the situation and unnerved by the unusual punishment. He struggled to his feet, he took a deep breath, then he followed his grandfather out of the basement.

Chapter Six

Settling In

In the living room, Ronald pointed at Malcolm's bag and said, "Grab your stuff. I forgot to mention this earlier, but it's very important: don't leave your shit on the floor. Not here, not there, not anywhere. Your grandmother and I are strong people, but no one can stop the... the 'effects' of aging. We're old, boy, and that's the truth. If we fall, that's it. We might never walk by ourselves again. It'd be canes and wheelchairs after that. So, clean up after yourself. Understood?"

"Yes, sir," Malcolm said as he grabbed the duffel bag from the floor.

Ronald examined his grandson with a set of narrowed eyes, curious. He recognized the fear pumping through Malcolm's body. He had seen that same fear in his peers before. Hollow-eyed and pale-faced, the boy stood with his head hanging down and his shoulders slumped. The bunker took a toll on him—or maybe it was just the rotten food.

Ronald pointed at the basement door and said, "Let me explain something to you, boy. I put you in there, in purgatory, for your own good. I did it to set our boundaries and to teach you something about discipline. I don't want you acting all pissy and spiteful because of that. Understood?"

Malcolm lifted his head and gazed into his grandfather's eyes. He stared down at him since the old man was a few inches shorter, but Ronald still managed to intimidate him. Malcolm had to fight the urge to strike him. He pictured himself hitting his grandfather with a backhanded slap, but he feared he would be overpowered afterward. He thought: *I can't believe it, I'm actually scared of a senior citizen.*

Ronald said, "Purgatory, the hole, whatever you want to call it... It's a tried-and-tested method for breaking men. It is a part of psychological warfare, it is a method of torture. Total isolation can break any man. Some might last longer than others, but, eventually, they all fall." He looked over at the basement door, his reminiscent eyes seeing into the past. He said, "I saw it during the war, son, but the prisoners got it far worse. They went days, *months,* without human contact in small huts and cages. And, when they were finally acknowledged, they were physically tortured. Many of them died painful deaths, but some of them survived. Oh, yes, some of them survived..."

Malcolm breathed deeply as he digested the horrific information. He barely met his grandparents, so he didn't know much about their pasts.

He asked, "Were you a soldier? Were you really in a war?"

Ronald quickly blinked five times, as if he had just snapped out of a trance. He said, "That's a story for another time. The point is: I put you in there to teach you and to test you. I wanted to make sure you weren't one of those new-age, sensitive pussies like the rest of your generation. Fortunately for both of us, you passed the test." He beckoned to Malcolm and said, "Follow me. I'll show you around."

Holding the duffel bag close to his chest, Malcolm followed Ronald to the kitchen. The kitchen was small and neat. A small round table sat at the center of the room. Counters with granite tops hugged the walls. A silver kettle and a pan sat on the stove while the sink was clean and empty. To the left of the stove, there was a door that led to the side of the house.

Malcolm wasn't surprised by the normality of the kitchen. He expected it in the house of his elders. He was, however, surprised by the window above the sink. Through the window, rays of orange sunshine poured into the room. The teenager thought: *it's already the afternoon. I really was in there for hours.*

Breaking Malcolm's contemplation, Ronald pointed at the two-door refrigerator and said, "Remember: no pillaging. We're not in Mexico, boy, we've got rules around here. You're free to come in here and sit down, but don't eat anything without asking your grandmother first." He pointed at another archway on the other side. He said, "If you go through there, you'll find yourself in the den, which is like the living room. Okay? There's only a sofa and some books in there, though, so feel free to sit down and read between your chores—*if* you can read English. You'll find a bathroom, a storage closet, and a door to the backyard through there, too. The backyard is nothing special, but you'll still be in charge of mowing it. You'll see all of that tomorrow while you're doing your chores. Now follow me."

Malcolm and Ronald returned to the living room.

Ronald said, "You're allowed to watch television,

but you must ask for permission first. You will have to work around our schedules. If our shows are on, you're going to have to wait. You're free to join us, but you better be respectful. I don't want you cackling like an animal. Understood?"

"Yes, sir."

"Good. Let's head upstairs."

Malcolm and Ronald ended up in a hallway on the second floor. There were two doors to the left, two doors to the right, and one door at the end.

Ronald explained everything to him. The first door to the left led to the guest bedroom while the second door led to the home office. On the right side of the hall, the first door led to a bathroom and the second door opened up to a staircase that led to the attic. The master bedroom was located at the end of the hall.

Ronald said, "You will not disturb us when our room is occupied. You will only enter our bedroom to complete your chores. You will not enter my office without permission, either, and you will *never* enter the attic. You're free to rest in your room or even take a 'fruity' bubble bath in the bathroom if that's what you like, but just stay out of our way." He opened the first door to the left and said, "This is the guest room. You'll be sleeping here during your stay."

Malcolm stood in the doorway and looked into the room. It was nothing special. There was a twin-sized bed under the window, the mattress dressed with plaid bed sheets. A nightstand with a lamp and a clock stood beside the bed. A dresser and a desk hugged the other walls. There was an empty closet, too. *At least it's not a bunker,* he thought, *no TV or computer, but I can survive in here.*

He walked lazily into the room and sat on the bed. He pulled his phone out of the duffel bag and started tapping and swiping.

Standing in the doorway, Ronald said, "We usually leave this room vacant and lend it to neighbors when times get rough. You know, cheating spouses, drunk husbands, pill-popping mothers, runaway teenagers... We cleaned it up for you, though. I hope you can appreciate that."

As he quickly tapped his phone, cycling through his social media apps, Malcolm said, "I do, sir."

Ronald coughed, then he said, "Hey, boy, give me your phone."

Malcolm stopped tapping. He slowly lifted his head and glared at his grandfather. The request was simple, but it sounded different to Malcolm. Asking him to give up his phone was like asking him to give up a testicle—it was a cruel and absurd request.

He smiled and said, "I think I'll keep it. I mean, I didn't notice any landline phones around the house. What if my mom tries to call me? What if I have to call her?"

"You don't have to worry about that, boy. We have cell phones around here. If she calls, we'll let you know. Now, *hand it over.*"

"I, um... No, I just can't do that. I need it, man. It's my only connection to the world, it's my only lifeline."

"Man? Did you just call me 'man?' You really don't learn, do you?"

Ronald let out a frustrated exhale. He closed his

eyes and ran his fingers through his slick hair. He was simultaneously amused and annoyed by his grandson's defiance. He took a deep breath, trying to keep his composure, then he opened his eyes.

He asked, "Do you want to go back to purgatory, boy?"

"N–No, but I can't give it to you. It's my phone, not yours."

"Don't kid yourself, boy. We both know you didn't pay for that phone. You and your spic gang probably stole it. If not, your mother bought it with the money your grandmother has been sending her."

Ronald slowly approached the bed, his hands on his hips. He gave Malcolm the opportunity to apologize and forfeit his phone while blocking the boy's escape route. He wasn't afraid of getting physical.

Malcolm tightened his grip on his cell phone and stared down at his lap. His grandfather's racism infuriated him. He was born and raised in Los Angeles, but he never experienced such candid and consistent racism. *This man is supposed to be family,* he thought, *but he's nothing but a racist bastard.* He gritted his teeth and shook his head, ready to take a stand.

He said, "Listen, old man, if you want this phone, you're going to have to take it from my cold–"

Mid-sentence, Ronald struck Malcolm with a powerful slap. The slap hit the left side of Malcolm's head, hitting his cheek, his forehead, and even his ear. Malcolm felt his teeth clash together, a *clinking* sound escaping his mouth upon impact. His left ear buzzed and stung for a few seconds. The left side of his face turned pink while his left ear reddened.

Malcolm rubbed his cheek and stared at his grandfather with wide eyes. He looked down at Ronald's right hand. It was a big, rough hand, but it looked normal. Yet, he felt like he was struck with a brick.

Ronald tightly gripped Malcolm's wrist, then he pried the phone from his hand. He shoved the phone into his pocket and walked back to the doorway.

Without looking back at his grandson, Ronald said, "Don't push me, boy. I'm not afraid of you, but you should be afraid of me. Do you understand me?"

His bottom lip quivering, Malcolm stuttered, "Y– Yes, sir."

"Good. Are you hungry?"

"No, sir."

"Then get some sleep. Breakfast is at six, but you'll be awake before that, won't you?"

"Yes, sir."

"After breakfast, we'll talk about your chores. Good night, boy."

Trying to control his rage, Malcolm croaked out, "Good night, sir."

Ronald walked out of the room and closed the door. Malcolm listened to his footsteps as his grandfather headed to the master bedroom. The sound of a door opening and closing seeped into the guest room—his grandfather was gone.

Malcolm grunted and threw a pillow at the door. Then he turned around and punched down at the mattress, releasing all of his bottled-up anger.

As he punched the bed, he muttered, "Shit, shit, shit. This isn't over. I'll get you back for this, old man..."

Chapter Seven

The First Night

Malcolm lay in bed, his fingers interlocked over his chest. He stared vacantly at the ceiling with glazed and somber eyes. Moonlight shone through the neighboring window, washing him with a milky glow, but the room was still dark. It was brighter than the bunker, though, and that was enough to comfort him.

The young teenager thought about his stay at his grandparents' house. *One day*—he was broken and beaten on the first day of his stay. He spoke to his grandparents for less than thirty minutes before he was pushed into the bunker, then he was slapped before he was sent to sleep. It was difficult to believe. An elderly man and his eagerly compliant wife—his own grandparents—abused him.

He whispered, "He said it was a method of torture, so he really tortured me. I can call the cops on them, I can show them 'the hole.' I'll probably have a bruise on my face, too. Yeah, I can get them arrested." He grimaced and shook his head. He whispered, "No, I can't. If I did, they'd arrest my mom, too, right? Hell, they'd arrest all of us, huh? Then again, maybe I can get some sympathy points if I call the police. I'll get out of trouble back home, that racist bitch will get arrested, and everything will go back to normal."

Malcolm cycled through the options. He evaluated

the risks and the rewards. In the best-case scenario, he figured he'd return home to his mother and suffer the consequences of his past actions. In the worst-case scenario, he believed his entire family would be arrested and he would be left alone— possibly in a jail cell. The best-case scenario seemed far more likely, though.

He whispered, "If I wanted to call the cops, I would need a phone. I don't have a phone because he took it. So, how do I get it back? How do I find it in this house? It's not like I could just go to the police station, either. I don't even know where it is. Damn it..."

He looked over at the window. He crawled closer to the wall and pushed the curtain aside, then he peered through the blinds. The street was calm. There were no trouble-making teenagers in sight, no homeless people loitering in the alleys, and no cars racing down the streets. There was a hell of a difference between the suburbs and the inner city.

Malcolm thought: *I could run away, I could just leave everything behind and start a new life.* He had considered that option before the incident at school. He couldn't abandon his mother, though.

He said, "I can't go without her. She put me in this place, but I still love her. Fuck it, whatever..."

He sighed and stood from the bed. He crept out of his room and glanced over at the master bedroom. The door was cracked open, allowing the sound of creaky wood to exit the room. *They're still awake,* he thought, *I wonder what they're doing in there?* It was an hour shy of midnight, but the house was still alive with faint noises. The noise in the bedroom could have been anything, but Malcolm wasn't eager to find out.

On his tiptoes, the teenager walked down the stairs. The stairs creaked and cracked and cried under his toes. He made his way to the kitchen. He opened a cupboard and found himself staring at bowls and plates. He opened another cupboard and —*voila!*—he found the cups. Cup in hand, he looked up at the ceiling and slunk towards the fridge.

The coast was still clear so he opened the refrigerator. Along with a cool breeze, a wave of light poured out of the fridge and illuminated the entire kitchen. Unfortunately, bottled water wasn't available at the O'Donnell household. Instead, the fridge was stocked with chicken breasts, ground beef, vegetables, fruit, and some condiments.

"I guess I'm drinking from the tap," Malcolm murmured.

He quietly filled his cup at the sink. He wasn't fond of tap water, but he was thirsty. As he chugged the water, he heard a deep, hoarse groaning sound. It sounded like a moan. He couldn't tell if it was a moan of pleasure or pain, though. He couldn't even tell if it was human. *It was a floorboard,* he thought, *the house is old, like them.*

After finishing the water, he dried the cup and returned it to the cupboard—*everything in the right place.*

He walked through the other archway and entered the den. The den was practically vacant, except for the three-seat couch at the center of the room and the bookcases hugging the walls. Shelves filled with old, musty novels, the den looked more like an ancient reading room than anything else.

Malcolm peeked into the backyard through the back door. The grass could use a trim, but it stood at an acceptable height. The grill, the patio table, and the lawn chairs were covered in dust and dirt, though. There hadn't been a family gathering or neighborhood barbecue at the O'Donnell house in years.

The teenager whispered, "They don't get much company, do they?" As he returned to the living room, he sarcastically said, "Gee, I wonder why..."

While reaching for the television remote, Malcolm heard the groan again. This time, he was certain it was human. He looked at the staircase with wide, protuberant eyes.

Just above a whisper, he said, "Grandma, is that you? Grandpa? Hello?"

There was no response, but he heard another moan. His curiosity got the best of him. He tiptoed up the stairs and returned to the second floor. In the hall, a constant *thumping* sound joined the moaning. Shoulders and heels raised, he crept towards the master bedroom, the possibilities running rampant in his mind.

He didn't know why the thought crossed his mind, but he believed Ronald was clubbing Barbara to death. A vivid image of his grandmother's bloodied, crushed head flashed in his mind.

Malcolm stopped in front of the door. He breathed quietly through his nose, mentally preparing himself for the worst. He pushed the door open an inch and peeked inside. He slapped his hands over his mouth and held his breath. His eyes practically popped out of his skull and his legs wobbled under him. He felt like his mind had melted, his confused thoughts blending together to create nothing but madness.

Ronald and Barbara were on the queen-sized bed. Barbara stood on all fours and faced the headboard while Ronald stood on his knees behind her. They were buck naked and they had sex in the doggy-style position.

Thanks to the moonlight entering the room through the window, Malcolm could see *everything.*

Ronald had a pair of thick arms and a bulky chest. His abs weren't defined like Malcolm's, but he looked strong. Barbara was fluffier than her husband. Her big, soft ass, the rolls of fat on her stomach, and her sagging breasts jiggled with each thrust, flesh rippling like waves at a shore.

Ronald thrust as hard and as fast as possible. He gripped an ass cheek with his left hand and tugged on her short hair with the other. Barbara, eyes squeezed shut, moaned and whimpered.

In a low voice, louder than a whisper but still soft and faint, Barbara said, "Fuck me, Ronnie. Oh, fuck me harder. You can do better than that, baby. Fuck me, Ronnie." Ronald tugged on her hair, causing her to yelp. Barbara sternly said, "*Harder.*"

Still thrusting, Ronald released his grip on her hair. He spanked her ass, cycling between cheeks as if he were playing the bongos. He hit her until her ass turned red, until little red dots formed on her skin—*petechiae*. The pain only aroused her, though. She tilted her head up and moaned with pleasure.

Ronald tightly gripped the nape of her neck and

leaned closer to her ear, still thrusting. He hissed, "Keep your voice down, you nasty little cunt. You trying to wake the boy or something?"

"Wake him. Let him watch."

"Shut your mouth or I'll fuck your asshole until you're split in two."

"Do it. Do it, Ronnie. Make me bleed."

Ronald was happy to oblige. He pulled out of her vagina, then he thrust into her asshole with all of his might. Barbara yelped as her limbs locked up. Then she giggled and shed tears of pleasure. She welcomed the pain with open arms.

Malcolm staggered away from the door, shaking his head in disgust and awe. He walked back to his room with wide lunges, then he quietly closed the door behind him. He covered himself with the blanket and wrapped the pillow around his head. He tightly closed his eyes and counted sheep, trying his best to fall asleep. Images of the rough sex and echoes of the dirty talk lingered in his mind, though.

He knew about sex, he took a sex education class and he watched porn, but it was different in the O'Donnell house. His grandparents' sex was fueled by deviance and anger. It was rough, violent, and *threatening*. It was the type of sex where people were either injured or killed—intentionally or unintentionally—during the act. It frightened him, and it kept him awake throughout the entire night.

Chapter Eight

Good Behavior

"What's wrong with you, boy?" Ronald asked. "You look like you haven't slept in weeks, but you've only been here for a day. You got something on your mind?"

Malcolm sat on the sofa in the living room, black bags hanging under his heavy-lidded eyes. He stared up at his grandfather, who stood near the recliner. He could also hear his grandmother in the kitchen, washing the morning's dishes.

Malcolm and Ronald had pancakes and milk for breakfast while Barbara ate warm oatmeal and berries with a cup of orange juice.

Malcolm had a lot on his mind, but he didn't know how to properly respond to Ronald's question. A daring response would be: *I accidentally caught you fucking my grandma while threatening to 'split her in two' through anal sex.* He wanted to avoid trouble, though, so he opted for the safest response.

He said, "No, sir. I've got nothing on my mind."

Ronald smirked and said, "Yeah, I thought so. You taco-heads don't have much for brains, do you? Well, I hope you're capable of listening, boy. I know we had some 'issues' last night, but today is a new day. This is your opportunity to prove you're more than just another fool in the world, this is your chance to prove yourself to me and... and to yourself, I suppose. Understood?"

"Yes, sir."

"Good, good. Now let's go over your chores. Your sweet grandmother is in the kitchen washing the dishes right now. She won't be doing that anymore. From now on, it is your responsibility to wash the dishes after every meal. Even if you don't eat, you better make those dishes spotless. After you wash the morning's dishes, you will make the beds in the guest room and the master bedroom. I want hospital corners, you hear me?"

Malcolm nodded in agreement. He had spent the previous summer at a juvenile boot camp for shooting a pellet gun at a 'friend,' so he knew all about hospital corners.

Ronald continued, "You will broom the living room, the kitchen, and the den every day. Don't worry about mopping. Like I said before, I don't want to fall and break a hip because of you. Your grandma doesn't want that, either. You will also mow the front lawn and backyard. I expect you to be finished with that by the weekend." A smug smile formed on his face. He said, "That shouldn't be too hard for you, though. Hell, your people are practically born with lawn mowers, aren't they? It's in your blood to mow these lawns. You know what else is in your blood? Plumbing and shit. You're going to be in charge of cleaning the bathrooms and unclogging the toilets. You hear me, boy?"

Malcolm gritted his teeth and clenched his fists. He imagined a scenario where he defeated his grandfather. He pictured himself punching Ronald's flabby stomach—his most vulnerable point. With the air knocked out of him, he would pull his grandfather's head down and he'd hit his face with his knee. Then, he would run out the front door and hitchhike back to Los Angeles.

Interrupting his fantasy, Ronald sternly repeated, "*You hear me?*"

Malcolm said, "Yes, sir."

From the kitchen archway, Barbara asked, "Doesn't that sound like too much for him, Ronnie? I don't mind doing the dishes."

"It's fine, Babs," Ronald said. "Chores teach kids about work. Some of those kids even get allowances, so it's just like work. But, you won't be getting an allowance, boy."

Malcolm responded, "So it's more like slavery?"

"That's a word for it, I suppose. I like to think of it like... like you're working in a communist country. You get nothing and I get everything. Okay? You youngsters really love praising communism these days, don't you?"

"I'm not a communist."

"Of course you're not..."

Barbara waved at Ronald and said, "Really, I don't mind doing the dishes."

Ronald said, "Stop it, Babs. He's not on vacation. He's being punished, remember? He broke the rules back home and now he's here. Now drop it and get back to what you were doing." As Barbara retreated to the kitchen, Ronald turned his attention to Malcolm and said, "You're young, but you're a man. You are a man, aren't you? A man should be able to handle these simple chores without complaining. Can you do that for us, boy? Hmm? Can you?"

Malcolm didn't care about labels. His grandfather

attempted to insult his masculinity, but he couldn't be manipulated in such a way. Still, he had to accept the chores or he would surely be punished.

He said, "I can handle it, sir."

"Good. Remember, you have until the weekend to mow those lawns. It better be finished by Sunday. Now, get started."

***

Malcolm spent two days—Friday and Saturday—completing chores at the O'Donnell house. On the first day, immediately after speaking to his grandfather, he marched up the stairs and made the beds. He successfully fought the urge to snoop around the master bedroom, although the nightstands called his name. They said: *we have secrets for you, Malcolm, take a peek*.

After making the beds, he headed downstairs and started sweeping the entire first floor. It took him two hours to broom the floors and dust every piece of furniture in the living room, kitchen, and den. Then, he spent another hour cleaning the bathroom and unclogging the toilet, which was clogged *before* his arrival at the house.

Eventually, lunchtime arrived and he shared another quiet meal with his grandparents. They ate turkey sandwiches and drank orange juice. Although Barbara insisted on washing the dishes again, trying to sneak one past the old man, Malcolm ultimately cleaned the mess after the meal in order to avoid trouble.

After lunch, Malcolm started working on the backyard. He dusted and scrubbed the old patio furniture, then he mowed the grass. He used a push mower—an old one without a motor—so it took his entire afternoon. He proved his grandfather wrong, though. He was, indeed, a 'man' who could handle his chores without complaining.

For dinner, the family ate meatloaf and mashed potatoes. Once again, Barbara tried to wash the dishes, but Ronald wouldn't allow it. So, Malcolm cleaned the kitchen until his grandfather was satisfied, then he retreated to his bedroom. He was finally finished with his chores for the day. He was finally free.

Freedom wasn't exactly 'fun' in the O'Donnell house, though.

Malcolm couldn't watch television in the living room, so he spent the afternoon in his bedroom. He lay in bed and stared up at the ceiling, lost in his thoughts. He didn't want to look out the window because it made him feel like a prisoner. He was, unfortunately, immune to the happiness that infected the whole neighborhood. Once again, he counted sheep until he dozed off.

On Saturday, Malcolm repeated the monotonous process while limiting his interactions with his grandparents. He ate breakfast, he washed the dishes, he made the beds, he swept the first floor, then he ate lunch and washed the dishes—*again.*

After lunch, he found himself in the front lawn with the push mower. The sun beating down on his neck, he pushed the mower from one end of the lawn to the other. Sweat dripped across his face, neck, and chest and a warm sensation flowed through his tired limbs. He wore a white wife beater, blue jeans, and sneakers. The shirt revealed his strong arms and lean chest while molding against the outline of his toned abs.

As he pushed the mower, Malcolm looked around the neighborhood. A few housewives sat on the porches of the neighboring houses, sipping wine and gossiping. Most of their husbands appeared to be out, except for a few elderly retired men who preferred to spend the weekends at home. Some children played tag on the street, others headed *away* from the neighborhood.

Malcolm spotted a group of teenagers on the other side of the street—two boys, two girls. The group stood in front of a two-story house, which eerily resembled the O'Donnell house. They appeared to be waiting for someone.

One of the girls caught his eye. Her short, dark auburn hair barely reached down to the back of her neck. She had freckles on her cheeks and nose, and a dimple on her left cheek with each smile. She had bright hazel eyes, too. She stood five-one and she wore a white blouse, denim shorts, and sandals.

The young woman waved at Malcolm, then she blushed and giggled. The other girl laughed with her, clearly amused. As they separated from the group, the girls yelled something along the lines of: *bye, we'll see you at the house.* The young men stayed behind.

As he watched the girls, Malcolm whispered, "There goes my chance with her..."

He looked over at the guys. A blonde-haired teenager gave him the finger and mouthed something at him. Malcolm couldn't read lips, but he bumped heads with dozens of bullies in his lifetime

—and, as if connected to a hive mind, they all shared the same vocabulary. So, he assumed the teenager mouthed something along the lines of: *you fucking faggot.*

The other teenager, a kid with bushy black hair, appeared to be taunting him, too. He smirked and nodded at Malcolm while mouthing a few hateful words.

Malcolm took a deep breath and glared at the teenagers. If he were at home, he would have vaulted over the fence and swung at them. The odds were stacked against him, but that was nothing new. Bumps and bruises didn't frighten him. Purgatory, on the other hand, terrified him. He couldn't take the risk, so he could only wait and glare.

He watched as a young man exited the house and joined the group. Instead of persuading the others to leave, he got in on it. He mouthed: *get out here, pussy.*

Under his breath, Malcolm murmured, "If it weren't for the old man, I would be beating your asses right now. I swear, I'm going to–"

He stopped upon spotting the sudden fear on their faces. Two of them shook their heads, the other stood motionless. They jogged down the sidewalk, shoving each other and muttering about something. *Ahem*—the faint sound emerged from the porch.

Malcolm instinctively glanced over his shoulder, then he gasped and hopped. He saw his grandfather standing on the porch, looking as intimidating as ever. Malcolm thought: *when the hell did he come out? Were those guys scared of him?*

Ronald said, "You've done well, boy. You finished

your chores, you stayed out of trouble... You proved that you can be trusted. I don't know if I can call you a 'man' just yet, but you're starting to look like one."

Still unnerved by his grandfather's sudden presence, Malcolm stuttered, "Tha–Thanks..."

"Your grandmother and I have decided to reward you for your cooperation. So, you'll have a 'free' day tomorrow. After your morning chores, you'll have four hours—from 1300 to 1700—to catch a movie and get some fresh air. You understand?"

"Yes, sir."

"So, what time will you be home tomorrow?"

"At five o'clock."

"Exactly."

Before Ronald could say another word, Malcolm asked, "Can I have my phone back?"

Ronald narrowed his eyes and curled his lips back in a snarl. The expression on his face said: *what the hell did you just say?*

Malcolm explained, "It's just so I can look for a cool place to rest and hang out. That's all."

"No," Ronald responded. "We'll give you directions to the plaza tomorrow morning. There's a theater and a few restaurants around there. We'll give you some money, too. We'll even give you enough to call us on a payphone if there's an emergency. You don't need your cell phone. You'll get your cell phone back when I feel like you've earned it. Understood?"

Malcolm sighed, then he said, "Yes, sir."

Ronald beckoned to him and said, "Good. Put the mower away and come inside. Dinner is almost ready."

Chapter Nine

Love at First Sight

The plaza was located in the downtown area of the small city, so naturally it was bustling with activity. Couples, young and old, held hands as they walked from shop-to-shop. Some children played tag and squirted each other with water guns at the neighboring park. Families strolled into the theater, excited to watch the latest movies.

Malcolm stood in front of the theater, eyes bright with curiosity. *This is too good to be true,* he thought, *there must be some sort of alien invasion going on around here.* Although some were disappointed and disgruntled, most of the civilians looked happy. They all seemed genial and helpful. It really was too good to be true.

He tried to shrug off the eerie vibe. He purchased a ticket for *Get Out,* directed by Jordan Peele, and he watched the movie. He spent around twenty minutes walking to the theater, ten minutes waiting for the movie to start, and another hundred minutes actually watching the film. So, after the movie, he still had an hour and fifty minutes before he had to head back to his grandparents' house.

As he stood in front of the theater, watching the happy patrons, Malcolm whispered, "I don't belong here. I'm not like these people and they're not like me. This place... I have to get out of this place."

He felt like he didn't belong. He was surrounded

by nice people, he knew his way around the neighborhood, but he still felt lost. The environment reminded him of the bunker in the basement, despite the significant differences.

He whispered, "I can't go home yet. I need to clear my mind, man."

Malcolm walked away from the plaza. He didn't know all of the streets, but he memorized his grandparents' neighborhood. He decided to take the long way home, walking along the outskirts of the city. He found himself in the impoverished side of town, surrounded by tumbledown houses. It still felt safe, though.

His eyes widened upon spotting a condemned house—one of many. The little blue house was rundown, burdened with boarded windows and tall grass, but it was perfectly habitable. He didn't care about the house, though. He cared about the girl pacing back and forth on the porch, chatting on her cell phone—the auburn-haired girl from the previous day.

Shit, shit, shit, Malcolm thought, *should I say something or should I keep walking?* With his shoulders raised, stiff like a flag pole, he awkwardly waddled past the house. He looked straight ahead while thinking about running across the street.

Before he could reach the neighboring house, the girl shouted, "Hey!"

Malcolm stopped and sighed. He slowly turned towards the house, then he pointed at himself, as if to say: *are you talking to me?*

The girl giggled, then she said, "Yeah, you. Come over here." As Malcolm opened the gate, the girl held the phone to her ear and said, "I'll call you back later, mom. Yeah... *Yes,* I'll be home at seven. Love you, too."

As she hung up the phone, Malcolm asked, "What's up?"

"What's your name?"

"Malcolm Hernandez."

"You're not from around here, are you, Malcolm?"

"No."

"So, where are you from?"

"Wait a minute. I told you my name, shouldn't you tell me yours?"

The girl huffed, then she said, "It's Claire—Claire Olson."

"Claire. That's a pretty name. Has anyone ever–"

"Don't bother with the pick-up lines," Claire interrupted. She walked down the porch steps and said, "Follow me. It's more comfortable in the back."

Malcolm watched as Claire nonchalantly opened a gate on the left side of the house. She beckoned to him, then she walked down a narrow path beyond the gate. Malcolm glanced around the neighborhood and thought about the situation. He feared Claire was leading him to a trap. *Those guys are back there,* he thought, *they're going to jump me, aren't they?*

He walked up to the gate and stared down the path. Claire had already entered the backyard, so he didn't have the chance to see her again. *I can still run,* he thought, *I can run home and stay out of trouble.* He wanted to avoid his grandfather's wrath, but he couldn't resist Claire's invitation. He walked down the path and entered the backyard.

Malcolm smiled in relief as he examined the

overgrown backyard. He spotted Claire sitting on a lawn chair. A brunette girl, the same age as Claire, sat on a chair beside her. A cooler sat on the floor between them. The scent of marijuana stained the backyard. The brunette girl happened to be holding a glass pipe in her right hand.

Claire asked, "You want a beer?"

As he took a seat on a lawn chair across from the girls, Malcolm responded, "Yeah, sure."

Claire threw him a can from the cooler. The moist can nearly slipped out of his fingers, but he caught it. He *snapped* the can open and took a swig.

Claire said, "This is my friend, Vivian Garcia."

Malcolm sighed with satisfaction after taking the swig, then he said, "It's nice to meet you, Vivian. I'm Malcolm."

"You want a toke?" Vivian asked, extending the pipe forward.

"Nah, not today. Thanks for the beer, though."

Claire asked, "So, Malcolm, where are you from? What are you doing here?"

Vivian asked, "What are you doing at that house? At Ronald's house?"

Malcolm furrowed his brow as he examined the girls and thought about their questions. Claire's questions were normal, but Vivian's questions were questionable. Therefore, they were *all* questionable. He wondered what they knew about his grandparents. They clearly knew his grandfather's first name while he hardly knew any of the elders in his old neighborhood.

Malcolm said, "I'm from LA. I was suspended from school a few days ago and I might get expelled and arrested. So, I'm hiding out here."

Smirking, Vivian said, "Oh, a bad boy. What'd you do? Blow up a toilet with a cherry bomb? Swing on the principal?"

"I shot my teacher," Malcolm said with a deadpan expression. The girls cocked their heads back, surprised. Malcolm grinned and said, "Shot him with a squirt gun."

The girls scoffed.

Vivian asked, "They suspended you for that?"

"Well, I kinda pretended it was a real gun at first, so... Yeah, I'm in trouble."

Claire asked, "Why here, though? Why are you staying at the O'Donnell house?"

"Because they're my grandparents."

Silence befell the backyard. Malcolm watched the girls with a raised brow. As he took another swig of his beer, he thought: *did I say something wrong? Or is there something on my face?* Vivian lit the pipe and took another puff. She needed to calm her nerves. Claire just stared at Malcolm. She clearly had something to say, but the words wouldn't come out.

Malcolm smiled and said, "Both of you look surprised. I just said they're my grandparents. What's the big deal?"

Claire loudly swallowed in order to clear her throat, then she said, "Your grandpa, Ronald O'Donnell... he's sort of a legend around here. He's... He's like a very, *very* scary urban legend." Malcolm leaned forward, his elbows on his knees—attentive and curious. Claire continued, "He's not afraid of putting his hands on people. You know what I mean? He *will* hit you. You could be a doctor, a priest, a cop, or... or the president and he'd still hit you. Kids, teens, adults, old people... None of it matters to him. If you break his rules, if he gets angry, he'll beat you. That's what he's known for. He's this neighborhood's boogeyman."

Vivian added, "They say he's slapped every single person in the city at least once."

Malcolm asked, "Has he... Has he hit you before?"

"When I was five, maybe six years old, I ran onto his front lawn to grab a ball or a Frisbee or something. But, Ronald doesn't like it when you step on his grass without his permission. So, he dragged me to his porch, threw me on his lap, and then he spanked me. I cried, I told my mom and dad, but they didn't do shit about it. They were scared of him."

"He spanked me, too. I was probably eight or nine, though," Claire said. She stared down at her lap and twiddled her thumbs, as if she were thinking about something. She said, "Other kids have gotten it worse. He once grabbed a boy's arm so hard that it *snapped.* You could even hear his arm break through the entire street. He almost got in trouble for that, but he lied his way out of it. Then, he kicked some guy's ass for playing his music too loud. That guy ended up moving, like, a month later. Supposedly, he has a–"

"Shit, I have to go," Vivian said as she stared down at her phone. She shoved the phone and pipe into her pockets. She smirked and said, "You better call me tonight, Claire. And you better not mess around with her, Malcolm. I'm serious."

Malcolm returned the smile and said, "I can't

promise anything."

As Vivian walked around the corner, Claire shouted, "Call me if I forget!"

Malcolm and Claire locked eyes for a second, then they blushed, giggled, and looked away. The silence in the backyard was awkward, but they clearly liked each other.

Claire beckoned to Malcolm and said, "Come on, sit over here. I feel lonely." She laughed, then she said, "Sitting all the way over there, I feel like I smell or something. I don't stink, do I?"

"No, no. I'll, um... I'll sit next to you. Yeah, no problem."

Malcolm moved and sat on Vivian's chair. He glanced over at Claire, grinning like a child with a secret. Claire blushed again, running her fingers through her hair and giggling. Once again, the backyard was silent. They both shared the same thought: *what do I say?*

Breaking the silence, Malcolm said, "So, I saw you yesterday across the street from my grandpa's house. You were giggling, weren't you?"

"I don't know. I guess so."

"What was so funny?"

Claire shrugged and said, "I don't know. I guess I just laugh when I see cute boys."

"Yeah? Well, I guess I just stare like an idiot when I see cute girls."

"You must have thought I was *really* cute 'cause you looked *really* stupid."

The couple laughed while scooting closer to each other. Their laughter slowly dwindled until it ended, leaving only the sounds of cars and children to dance with the wind. They locked eyes again, like long lost lovers who finally found each other.

Without breaking eye contact, Claire said, "I... I think I like you."

"I like you, too," Malcolm responded, staring at her as if he were hypnotized by her eyes.

"Should we... kiss?"

"Yeah, I think that's a good idea."

Their noses clashed as they leaned towards each other. They shared a kiss. Malcolm caressed the back of Claire's neck, Claire gripped Malcolm's bicep and shoulder. The kiss started off sloppy—lips smacking, tongues wrestling, slobber dripping. It eventually became tame, clean, and heartfelt. There was a pinch of love in the kiss.

Malcolm and Claire found each other attractive, but they weren't controlled by teenage hormones or lust. They only knew each other for less than a day, but they truly cared about one another. It was called: *love at first sight.* They pulled away from the kiss and laughed, rosy-cheeked.

Claire said, "That was, um... nice."

Smiling, Malcolm said, "Yeah, it was good... I was good, right?"

"Yeah, I like that thing you did with your tongue," Claire said.

Malcolm flicked his tongue and widened his eyes, as if to say: *that thing?*

Claire said, "Yeah, that." She laughed and shook her head, tickled by his playful behavior. She said, "We should hang out again."

Malcolm sighed, then he responded, "I want to, but I don't have my phone right now. My grandpa took it away from me."

"Yeah, I thought he'd do something like that. I can get you a burner, though."

"A burner?"

"Yeah. You know, a cheap prepaid phone with some minutes and unlimited texting. It'll cost me some money, but I can get my hands on one."

"Really? That would be great. I mean, um... How much would I owe you?"

"Not much. You can just pay me back with... with a fancy dinner, some jewelry, a bouquet of roses, and a box of chocolate. Okay?"

Malcolm stared at her with a steady expression. He could buy his own replacement phone with that type of money.

Claire giggled, then she said, "I'm kidding. Don't worry, I'll hook you up. I've got connections."

"Cool, cool," Malcolm responded. He took a swig of his beer, then he said, "I really appreciate it, Claire. Like, I appreciate you and I appreciate... all of this. Being out here by myself, I was starting to feel like an alien. I felt like I didn't belong. Thanks for clearing my head."

"No problem, Malcolm. I know how you feel, too. I moved here when I was five and I felt the same. I think it's normal, but it'll get better. It just takes a little bit of time."

"Yeah, I'm feeling better already. I think–"

He stopped and stared vacantly at the grass, eyes and mouth wide open. One word echoed through his mind: *time.*

Claire snapped her fingers and asked, "What's wrong? Are you good? You're not going to throw up, are you?"

"What time is it?"

Claire checked her phone and said, "It's, um... 5:10."

"Shit, the old man is going to kill me. I have to go," Malcolm said. He kissed Claire, then he said, "I'll meet you here in a few days."

As Malcolm ran off, Claire stood up and shouted, "Okay, I guess! Bye!"

Chapter Ten

The Punishment

The sun had already fallen beyond the horizon, painting the sky black with streaks of blue and orange. Dark clouds hovered above the city, pouring down on the streets and soaking the lingering civilians with a soft drizzle. Some children played in the rain while the teenagers and adults rushed to their homes.

Holding his windbreaker jacket over his head, Malcolm quietly pushed the front gate open. He carefully closed the gate, then he made his way to the front porch with wide, silent lunges.

As he wiped his shoes on the doormat and stared at the door knob, he whispered, "Please be open, please be open, *please be open.*"

He wasn't given a key, so if the door wasn't open, he would either have to knock or find another way to sneak in. He grimaced as he grabbed the door knob. He took a deep breath, then he exhaled, then he took another deep breath. He twisted his wrist— and the knob moved with his hand. *Holy shit, it's actually open,* he thought, *they must have forgotten all about it, they're probably already asleep.*

Malcolm opened the door a few inches and peeked into the house. He could see into the living room. The lights were off, but he could see the staircase to the right. He slunk into the house, then he slowly and carefully closed the door behind him

—*so far, so good.* As he examined the locks, he thought: *should I lock up or let them get robbed?* He seriously considered the second option.

Click—the sound was quickly followed by a wave of light that illuminated the living room.

"Where have you been, boy?" a man asked.

Malcolm chewed on his bottom lip and stared absently at the front door, slightly dumbfounded. He didn't have to turn around to know who was waiting for him. The voice belonged to his grandfather. He safely assumed Ronald sat in the dark and waited for him. *Just like in the movies,* he thought, *I should have known better.*

He sighed and turned around. As expected, Ronald sat on the recliner, holding the knob of the lamp on the end-table. Barbara sat on the sofa, rubbing her eyes and yawning as if she had just awakened from a nap.

Ronald said, "Don't play dumb now. Answer the damn question, boy. Where have you been? Why are you late?"

Malcolm responded, "I lost track of time. I don't have a watch or a phone. What did you expect?"

"Don't talk back to me."

"I'm not talking back. I'm just answering your question."

"You're sassing me, boy. 'What did you expect?' What kind of bullshit answer is that?"

Malcolm lowered his head and said, "It's the truth."

"This city is filled with people with watches and phones. There ain't a single kid over thirteen that doesn't have a damn cell phone these days. Why couldn't you ask someone for the time? Huh?"

"I tried to ask, but... but they ignored me. You know, they gave me the cold shoulder."

Her back to Malcolm, Barbara shook her head and said, "No, no, no. That doesn't sound right, little Malcolm. This is a *wholesome* city filled with good, sweet people. If you ask for a hand, they'd give you an arm. Anyone would have given you the time... unless you were out there misbehaving and such."

Malcolm said, "Oh, come on. I just went out and watched a movie. That's it."

"Bullshit," Ronald said. "If that were true, you wouldn't have been late. Four hours is more than enough time to watch a movie and walk home. I know that for a fact. And, if you really didn't know the time, you wouldn't have known you were late and you wouldn't have been trying to sneak in here like a damn burglar."

Malcolm clenched his jaw and ran his fingers through his hair. He was pushed into a corner. He had lied his way through trouble before, but his grandfather was unbeatable.

Trying to think of an excuse, he stuttered, "I–I just... I looked at the sky. I saw that it was getting dark, so I... so I came home as fast as possible. I didn't *know* I was late, I just *thought* I was late. That's all."

Ronald scowled and said, "You're a bullshitter, kid, just like your punk father. Come here, boy. You need to be disciplined."

Malcolm furrowed his brow and responded, "What? No, it was an accident. You can't 'discipline' me for that, man."

"Get your ass over here before I get real angry."

Malcolm could already feel the anger in his grandfather's voice. He looked over at his grandmother, but she didn't seem interested. *Discipline*—in the O'Donnell house, the word could mean anything. His grandfather could slap him in the face or force him into the bunker for hours. He could even do something worse. The possibilities were endless and horrific.

Malcolm said, "I won't break the rules again, but I can't let you lock me up or hit me or abuse me. I'm... I'm just going to go to my room. Okay?"

He slowly walked past the sofa, stiff and frightened. He strolled past the recliner and approached the staircase. He could see the finish line—the top of the stairs.

As he stepped on the first stair, Ronald grabbed the nape of Malcolm's neck. His hand was rough and his grip was tight. His grandfather grabbed him from behind, but Malcolm felt as if he were being strangled from the front. He lost his balance, teetering left and right as Ronald pulled him back into the living room.

Malcolm reached for Ronald's wrist and shouted, "Let me go! What the fuck, man? Let me go!"

Ronald sat down on the recliner and brought Malcolm down with him. He laid Malcolm over his lap, face down and bottom up. He pushed his left elbow into the small of Malcolm's back, pinning him down so that he wouldn't escape.

Malcolm thrashed about, but to no avail. He felt his grandfather's sharp knees digging into his abdomen.

Ronald said, "Give me the paddle, Babs. It's time to teach this boy a lesson."

Malcolm stopped flailing his limbs upon hearing those words. From the corner of his eye, he watched as his grandmother retrieved a small wooden paddle from under the sofa. The paddle had a short handle and a wide blade, thick and sturdy. She handed the paddle to her husband with a smile. Malcolm thought: *they were always going to beat me, they wanted this, they're crazy.*

Ronald lifted the paddle over his head, then he swung down at Malcolm's ass. Malcolm flinched and let out a short scream—*ow!* Ronald struck him again, the *whoosh* of the swing echoing through the house. Malcolm bounced on his grandfather's knees and unleashed another scream—a louder, raspier shout.

Through his gritted teeth, Ronald said, "Take it like a man. The more you scream, the more I beat you. You hear me, boy?"

Malcolm shouted, "Yes!"

Ronald hit him again and barked, "Then stop screaming!"

Malcolm pulled his lips into his mouth and whimpered, tears glistening in his eyes. His faint cries were masked by the sound of the paddle whacking his ass. One, two, three... *ten*—Ronald spanked Malcolm ten more times with the paddle.

The pain in his tailbone increased with each hit. The pain caused him to sweat like a marathon runner. He felt a fuzzy sensation across his spine and even in his brain. Then, a frightening numbness began to set in. He still felt some pain with each spank, but it didn't last long.

He thought: *am I paralyzed? Is he really hitting me that hard?*

Exerting all of his energy, Malcolm gripped the side of the recliner and pushed himself away from his grandfather. He slipped past Ronald's elbow and fell to the floor between the chair and the coffee table. On all fours, he quickly crawled across the living room until he reached the dining area. He rubbed his ass and hissed in pain as he struggled to his feet. The slightest movement caused the greatest pain.

He stared at his grandparents in disbelief. Ronald and Barbara remained seated. Ronald breathed deeply through his nose, exhausted from the brutal beating he inflicted on his grandson. Barbara appeared to be confused, baffled by her grandson's defiance. They didn't seem remorseful, though.

Teary-eyed, Malcolm said, "I want my phone. I need to call my mom. *Now.*"

Ronald said, "First of all: watch your tone. I don't care if you're angry, you better show some respect to your elders." He handed the paddle to Barbara, then he shuffled in his seat to get comfortable. He said, "Your mother is busy dealing with your other disciplinary problems back home. I can tell she's going to have trouble convincing them to spare you. Shit, boy, this is barely your fourth day here and you've already got me spanking you. Besides, your mother is also busy working to keep food on the table so she doesn't have time to talk to you."

"I've been staying up-to-date with her, sweetheart. You don't need to talk to her," Barbara said.

Malcolm wiped the tears from his eyes and, with his voice cracking, he said, "You... You can't treat me like this. You can't just abuse me like this! It's illegal! I can call the cops!"

"What did I say about your tone?" Ronald asked, furious. Malcolm took a step back and clenched his jaw. Ronald said, "Listen to me, boy, and listen very carefully. The day you call the police to my house will be the worst day of your miserable, *pathetic* life. You will regret it. You won't just get a spanking with that little paddle, either. No, boy, no. I have a 'special' paddle for bastard kids like you. I have other 'tools,' too. Break the rules again and you'll see what I'm capable of. Understood?"

Malcolm couldn't say a word. He spotted the evil in his grandfather's eyes. His threats were sincere and terrifying. In the living room, he realized that he could possibly die at his grandparents' house.

Ronald repeated, "Understood?"

Malcolm stuttered, "Y–Yes, s–sir."

"Good. Now get your ass to bed. You're grounded for a day."

Malcolm watched as his grandfather casually turned on the television and flipped through the channels. Tears dripped from his eyes with each blink, he was emotionally and physically hurt, but his grandparents acted like everything was normal. He let out a broken sigh, then he retreated to his room—traumatized and defeated.

Chapter Eleven

Grounded

Malcolm lay in bed and stared at the ceiling, a soft pillow under his bruised ass. He had already eaten breakfast and finished the morning's chores. He spent the morning washing the dishes, making the beds, and sweeping the floors. So, he took a break before lunch. He thought about the beating during the previous night as well as his uncertain future.

He whispered, "What am I going to do? Should I fight back? Should I try calling my mom? Or can the cops actually help?" He grimaced in pain as he sat up in bed. He stared at the empty street—it was a school day—and he said, "I can still run away. He's stronger than me, but he's not faster... or is he?"

He checked the time on the vintage alarm clock. It read: *12:07*. Lunchtime had finally arrived.

Malcolm groaned and climbed out of bed. He shambled out of his bedroom and headed downstairs. As he entered the living room, he heard two faint voices coming from the kitchen—two male voices. He furrowed his brow as he crept up to the archway. He peeked into the kitchen, confused and curious, and then the voices stopped.

Ronald sat at one end of the kitchen table. Austin Williams, Ronald's neighbor and friend, sat across from him. The men glared back at Malcolm, scowling as if he had just ruined a great joke.

Austin was a middle-aged man, pushing fifty with

a steamroller. Like Ronald, however, he had a bulky physique. He could easily overpower Malcolm or any other teenager on the block.

Ronald said, "Malcolm, this is my good friend Austin Williams. You will address him as 'sir' or 'Mr. Williams.' He lives right across the street."

With a deep, almost frightening voice, Austin said, "It's nice to meet you, son."

Malcolm nodded reluctantly and stuttered, "It– It's nice to meet you, too, sir."

Ronald said, "Your grandmother and I will be running errands today. We have to buy groceries, pick up some medicine, and that sort of stuff. So, you'll be staying here alone. *But,* Austin has agreed to watch our house from his place. I've also asked some of our other kind neighbors to inform me if they see you out on the streets." He leaned forward, elbows on the table. He said, "We might not be home, but we still have rules. You better not break any of them. And, remember, you're grounded. You're already in trouble, boy, and you don't want to dig yourself any deeper. Believe me when I say that."

Malcolm nodded in agreement. He felt like he didn't have any other options. He watched as Ronald and Austin spoke and laughed. He could see their lips flapping, mists of saliva escaping their mouths with each cackle, but he didn't hear a sound. He only thought about the beating—thump, thump, *thump.*

Unable to control himself, Malcolm shouted, "He beats me!" He nodded and said, "Yeah, you heard me. My grandpa beats me! He slapped me the other night and he beat my ass with a paddle yesterday! I... I can barely sit down! He beats me!"

A dead silence filled the kitchen. Malcolm stared at Ronald, then he looked over at Austin, begging for help with a pair of puppy eyes. The men stared back at him, bored and emotionless. Ronald huffed, then he chuckled. Austin looked over at him and joined in on the laughter.

Malcolm opened his mouth to speak, but he couldn't say a word. He could only croak and groan. He thought: *what is wrong with this place? These people are all crazy.*

Smiling, Austin said, "Of course he beats you, son. You broke his rules, didn't you? He's your grandfather and he has the *right* to punish you. Corporal punishment may be frowned upon by some delicate snowflakes, but it's not wrong or illegal."

Ronald said, "I'm telling you, Austin, this new generation has gone pussy on us. I hit the boy, sure, but I made sure I didn't cripple him. He should be grateful for that, right?"

"Right."

"These kids... They're not going to survive in the real world, are they? Sooner or later, the bubble is going to pop. When it's gone, it's gone. We need real men and real women in this world. That's what we need. I want this boy to be a real man."

Ronald and Austin continued talking about 'real' men, but Malcolm didn't hear them. He was awed by Austin's swift dismissal of his serious allegation. He expected a heartless response from his grandfather, but he hoped to receive some sympathy from Austin. *All of the adults in this whole damn city are insane,* he thought, *I'm going to need Claire's help if I want to get out of here.*

Ronald said, "Hey, boy." Malcolm glanced over at his grandfather, pulled out of his fear-induced trance. Ronald said, "I know you tried to hurt me by opening your big mouth, but I won't punish you for it. You gave us a good laugh and I appreciate that. Just remember: you better start showing some respect if you know what's good for you."

"He's right," Austin said. "You should always respect your elders. And your grandfather is a respected member of this community and a war hero. That should mean something to you, son."

Barbara approached the kitchen from behind Malcolm, a purse slung over her shoulder. She said, "I'm ready to go, Ronnie. How about you?"

Ronald responded, "I've been ready. Let's go."

As the men stood from their seats, Barbara rubbed Malcolm's shoulder and said, "I left a sandwich for you on the counter. Feel free to treat yourself to some juice or water." She leaned closer to his ear and whispered, "Go ahead and eat as much as you'd like, hun. I've got your back."

Ronald slipped into his leather jacket, then he patted Barbara's ass and nodded, as if to say: *let's get going.* Austin followed their lead.

From the front door, Ronald looked back at Malcolm and said, "You're grounded, boy. Don't forget that."

"Don't worry about him. I'll watch the place," Austin said on his way out.

The front door slammed shut and the adults departed from the house.

Malcolm dropped his arms to his sides and said,

"Shit."

***

Malcolm ate his sandwich, then he spent an hour completing his chores. He washed the dishes, scrubbed the bathroom, and dusted the furniture on the first floor. It was a dull but easy day. After his chores, he walked back to the living room and stared at the front door. He expected his grandparents to barge into the house, bags full of groceries and pills in their arms.

There was no sign of his grandparents' return, though.

Malcolm whispered, "What do I do now?"

He looked over at the kitchen archway. He could enjoy a snack, gnaw on some fruit or slurp some jello, but he wasn't hungry. He glanced over at the staircase. A dangerous, foolish, and downright stupid idea crept into his mind. He thought: *I can explore the house, I can find my phone, I can gain the advantage against them.* He took one final glance at the door, then he dashed up the stairs.

He ran down the hall, then he skidded to a stop in front of the master bedroom. He pushed the door open and leaned into the room.

At first glance, the master bedroom resembled every other plain bedroom on the planet. There was a large queen-sized bed towards the center of the room with nightstands on each side. There was a closet beside the bed. To the left, there was a six-drawer dresser. To the right, there was a desk and a full-body mirror.

Malcolm entered the room, his shoulders and heels raised. He gripped the knobs on a drawer with his fingertips, then he pulled it open. He found himself staring at his grandfather's underwear and socks. He gently pushed the underwear with the back of his hand and searched for anything unusual or useful. *Nothing,* he thought, *just some tighty-whities and some ripped socks.*

He opened the drawer to his right and sneered in disgust. He found his grandmother's pantyhose and panties. He decided to avoid that drawer. He opened the others, riffling through socks, undershirts, t-shirts, pens and pencils, balls of yarn, and other useless knick-knacks. His phone was nowhere in sight, though.

He closed the last drawer, then he looked around the room. The closet was open, so he could see into it from afar. Clothing hung from the pole and shoe boxes sat on the ground. It was normal.

"The nightstands," he whispered.

He approached the nightstand to the left and opened the top drawer. A bible, a rosary, some loose change, and a set of knitting needles were stored in the drawer—nothing of interest. He closed it, then he opened the other one. His eyes widened, his jaw dropped, and, for a moment, he felt like his heart stopped.

The drawer stored a trove of sex toys. A clear jelly dildo, a vibrating wand, a set of anal beads, a cock ring, and a butt plug sat in the drawer. The jelly dildo appeared to be glistening, too. Although he certainly didn't want it in his head, one thought dominated his mind: *did my grandma just use that?* He shuddered and sighed, disgusted.

He closed the drawer with his knee and shook his

head, trying his best to shrug it off. The image of the sex toys clung to his mind, although he tried to bury it in the deepest crevice of his brain. He approached the other nightstand—his grandfather's. *No sex toys, please no sex toys,* he thought.

He opened the drawer and muttered, "Shit."

The top drawer was nearly vacant. It stored a tattered, coverless novel—something from a used book store, surely—a necklace, some coins, and piles of dust. A box of magnum-sized condoms also sat in the corner of the drawer.

Malcolm snickered, then he whispered, "Come on, old man, you don't need condoms. You're not going to get her pregnant in your eighties." He closed the drawer and muttered, "Magnums... He's probably not even that big."

He froze before he could completely open the bottom drawer. He spotted the handle of a revolver. He glanced over his shoulder, then he looked down at the floor and listened. The coast was still clear.

He slowly pulled the revolver out of the drawer. He had fiddled with guns—fake and real—when he was younger. He thumbed the cylinder release latch, then he pushed the cylinder out. It wasn't loaded.

"Shit," Malcolm whispered. "I can't even scare 'em with this. It's no good without bullets."

He rolled the cylinder back into place, then he returned the revolver to the drawer—exactly where he found it.

Malcolm exited the room, quietly closing the door behind him. His grandparents still weren't home. He glanced over at the door to his right, then at the door to his left. He had two options: the office or the attic. *The creepier stuff will be in the attic, right?*–he thought.

He opened the door to his left. The staircase was dark, solely illuminated by the light in the hallway, but it was enough to see the attic above. He walked up the steps, grimacing as each stair creaked and howled. At the top of the stairs, a thick darkness enveloped him.

"Light," he whispered. "I need light."

He spotted a beaded pull chain dangling from the ceiling in front of him. He tugged on the dusty chain, causing a bulb to illuminate the attic with a yellow light. The shadows retreated to the corners of the room and he could finally see.

Malcolm muttered, "Holy shit."

***

The attic felt like a time capsule, filled with old furniture, tattered cardboard boxes, and war memorabilia. Cobwebs and dust clung to everything in the attic while spiders skittered across the walls and floors. The heavy furniture—dressers, chests, bookcases, and racks—hugged the walls while stacks of cardboard boxes formed aisles down the center of the attic.

As he approached a corner of the room, crouching under the cobwebs, Malcolm whispered, "I feel like I just went back in time. This is crazy."

He stopped before he reached the stack of cardboard boxes in the corner. He spotted a uniform display case on the wall to his left, the glass covered in smudges and dust. A military uniform hung in the case, but it was difficult to see.

"He was in a war," Malcolm said as he glided his

fingertips across the glass. "I wonder where he served. Korea? Vietnam? Afghanistan?"

Malcolm moved towards the stack of cardboard boxes. He found stacks and stacks of letters. All of the letters were addressed to Ronald. They appeared to be sent from Ronald's parents, friends, and girlfriends—more than one. None of the letters were sent by or addressed to Barbara. They were war letters. Unfortunately, the ink had faded away and the handwriting was illegible, so he couldn't read them.

He returned the letters to the box, then he picked up a stack of Polaroid photographs. He took two steps back and held the photos up to the light. Then he gasped and trembled.

Malcolm muttered, "What the fuck?"

He recognized his grandfather in the pictures—a young Ronald O'Donnell. Ronald's black hair was slicked back and his dark stubble spread from his face to his neck. The sinister look in his eyes had already developed. He smiled smugly in all of the pictures, proud of his immoral, deviant actions. The pictures depicted Ronald pillaging villages in Vietnam.

In one picture, he laughed as he set a hut on fire with a torch, the distorted figures of screaming children standing at the windows. In another photograph, grinning from ear-to-ear, he appeared to be raping a teenage Vietnamese girl. From the hollow look in her eyes, the girl was possibly dead at the time of the rape. It was too difficult to tell, though.

In other pictures, he posed with dead bodies and

decapitated heads. He even appeared to be erecting a decapitated head on a spike in another photo, giving a warning to his enemies in the country.

Hands trembling with fear, Malcolm blinked rapidly and said, "Oh, shit. Oh, fuck. Oh, shit!"

He returned the photos to their rightful place, then he closed the cardboard box. He stopped moving as he turned to leave. He spotted more furniture to his right. It wasn't normal furniture, though.

Wide-eyed, he said, "He's actually crazy. This... This isn't right. Why would he have this? Does he... Does he actually *torture* people up here?"

Malcolm had stumbled upon an arsenal of tools used for torture. He spotted an old, sturdy pillory. The pillory was customized so it could be bolted to the ground and the horizontal post could be raised and lowered. Beside the pillory, a tall, rusty cage leaned against the wall. It looked at least six feet long, two-and-a-half feet wide, and two feet deep, and one of the long sides was missing.

Several paddles leaned against the corner on the other side of the room. Some of the paddles had long handles, others were cut short. Long, rusty nails protruded from the blade of one of the paddles.

As he stared at the nail-paddle, Malcolm said, "He *does* torture people. Why would he have that if he didn't torture people? Shit, he could use that on me." He took two steps back and looked every which way. He stuttered, "He–He's not a collector, he's not selling this shit. N–No, this is *his* stuff. He's a psycho. He's going to–"

The sound of a car door slamming seeped into

the attic. The sound was followed by a set of muffled voices—Ronald, Barbara, and Austin.

They're home, Malcolm thought, *they can't catch me here.* He turned off the light and strode across the attic on his tiptoes, trying to avoid the creaky floorboards, then he daintily walked down the stairs. He stepped into the hall and closed the door behind him. To his utter relief, his grandparents were still outside.

Malcolm swiped at the sweat on his brow with the back of his hand. He took several deep breaths and calmed his nerves. He tried to crack a smile, then he frowned, and then he twisted his face into a neutral expression. *Act normal,* he thought, *don't do anything stupid.* He headed down the stairs and stood behind the recliner.

The front door swung open.

"Hey, Malcolm," Barbara said, two brown bags filled with groceries in her arms. "How was your day? Hmm? You ready to help me with dinner?"

Malcolm said, "Sure, sure."

Ronald entered the house, holding two plastic bags in his right hand and a brown bag in his left arm. He stood near the door and stared at his grandson. Five, ten, fifteen, *twenty seconds*—twenty seconds of dead silenced passed before he finally said a word.

Ronald said, "I spoke to Austin."

Malcolm clenched his jaw and nodded, as if to say: *okay, go on.*

Ronald smirked and said, "He said he didn't hear a peep from you. Looks like you cleaned the place up, too. That's good. That's real good."

"Thank you, sir."

"Listen up, boy. I'm not going to apologize for disciplining you, I didn't do anything wrong after all, but I will congratulate you for your hard work. I'll be honest: I expected nothing but defiance from you today and you proved me wrong. So, we're going to start fresh tomorrow. You'll have another day off, another chance to prove yourself. Think of it as a test—a test you don't want to fail. Understood?"

"I understand, sir."

"Good," Ronald said. He walked to the kitchen and said, "Now, come help your grandmother in the kitchen."

Malcolm watched his grandfather until he disappeared around the archway. He heard his grandparents' faint voices in the kitchen, but it didn't matter to him. He glanced up at the ceiling and thought about the revolting photographs and the tools of torture. He thought: *I have to follow the rules until I find a way out of here.*

He walked to the kitchen, ready to help his grandmother.

Chapter Twelve

Irresistible

Malcolm wanted to follow his grandfather's rules, but he couldn't resist Claire's allure. There was something about breaking the rules that always excited him, too. So, he spent around two and a half hours at the park, then he headed to the condemned house in the poor side of town—anxious, frightened, *excited.*

He's going to beat me if I'm late again, but I have to get the upper hand, he thought, *please be here, Claire.*

He walked through the front gate, glancing over his shoulder with every other step. He hoped none of his grandfather's friends—or spies—spotted him in the neighborhood. He walked down the narrow path at the side of the house, but he stopped before he could enter the backyard. He heard someone back there, shuffling about.

Under his breath, barely negligible, he murmured, "Please be Claire, please be Claire."

Malcolm walked around the corner. He couldn't help but sigh in relief. Claire sat on one of the lawn chairs, tapping and swiping at her cell phone. A backpack sat on the floor between her feet.

Malcolm smiled and said, "Claire."

Claire looked up from her phone. She smirked as soon as she spotted Malcolm. She saw him on Sunday and it was barely Tuesday, but it felt like weeks since they last met. They had a strong connection. The couple kissed—a quick peck on the lips—then they shared a tight hug.

Malcolm looked away from Claire as he sat down on the chair beside her. He still felt the pain on his ass from the paddling so he didn't want her to see his grimace. After adjusting to the pain, he glanced over at Claire, he smiled, and he nodded. He looked as if he had something to say, but he couldn't find the words to say it.

Breaking the silence, Claire said, "It feels like forever since the last time I saw you. How are things at your grandpa's house?"

Malcolm responded, "It's... shitty. I don't like it there. I just... I don't know what to say. It's just really shitty right now."

The backyard became silent as Claire watched him with glistening, concerned eyes.

Malcolm sighed, then he said, "Where's Vivian?"

Claire huffed, then she asked, "Why are you asking? You like her or something?"

"No. I mean, she's cool and chill and all that, but she's not as cool as you."

Claire rolled her eyes and snickered, amused by Malcolm's sweet talk.

Malcolm said, "I was just wondering 'cause I didn't expect to see you here alone. You're usually together, aren't you?"

"Yeah, but she had detention after class—*again.* I usually wait for her at school, but... Well, I wanted to see you without Vivian and I knew you'd show up here eventually."

"Damn, you must really like me, huh? My mom

always told me I was handsome, but I didn't know I was *that* good-looking."

"You're cute, but don't let it get to your head. It's not like you're DiCaprio in Titanic or anything like that."

The pair chuckled, then they kissed. Malcolm caressed Claire's cheek and neck while Claire stroked his jaw. They pulled away and gazed into each other's eyes.

Claire said, "I like you because you're not like the other guys. I don't know why, but... you're different. You're a 'troublemaker,' but you're kind, too. You're a breath of fresh air in this city—in my life. That's why I like you, Malcolm."

Malcolm continued to gaze into her bright, beautiful eyes. He knew she wasn't lying. He couldn't think of the words to respond, though. Only three words echoed through his head: *I love you.* His emotions were sincere, but it was too soon to utter those significant words. He didn't want to scare her off after all.

Claire reached into her backpack and said, "I brought you something." She pulled a touchscreen cell phone out of the bag—a Chinese knockoff. She handed the phone to Malcolm and said, "Here. It has two-hundred minutes and unlimited texting for a month. I already put my number in it so you can text me whenever you want. Just make sure you keep it on 'silent' so Ronald doesn't hear it. And, if you get caught, *please* don't tell him you got it from me."

Malcolm said, "He won't find a thing. Thanks, Claire. This is going to change everything. I can–"

He grimaced and hissed in pain. He felt a twinge

in his tailbone, the pain reverberating across his spine. He leaned onto his side, moving his weight away from his ass.

Claire asked, "What's wrong? Are you okay?"

Rosy-cheeked due to the pain and embarrassment, Malcolm looked down at the ground. *I have to tell her the truth,* he thought, *I have to get this off my chest.*

Without making eye contact, he said, "He beat me. The old man beat me."

Wide-eyed, Claire asked, "Really?"

"I got home late on Sunday. I didn't think it was a big deal, but... he obviously made it into a big deal. He grabbed me, he threw me over his legs like a kid, then he hit me with a paddle. He fucking spanked me, Claire, and I couldn't do anything to stop him. I just took it, then I went to my room, just like a little bitch. I should have hit him..."

"Damn. I really wish I could help, but it's hard. Ronald is... He's respected around here. He's like an abusive but 'talented' pop star: he's an asshole to everyone, he won't think twice about hitting someone, but people still like him for whatever reason. And, everyone knows not to fuck with him."

"I know. I noticed that yesterday. I told some guy, Austin Williams, about my grandpa beating me and he just laughed. He said it was my grandpa's right to beat me."

Claire smiled thinly—the smile of an unemployed person who was just rejected by another employer.

She said, "Mr. Williams... He's a lot like Ronald. He doesn't beat the neighborhood kids, he doesn't have the balls for that, but he beats on his family. My mom told me he hits his wife and kids when he gets drunk. Everyone knows about it. So, Williams isn't going to say a thing to Ronald about hitting you. An asshole won't criticize another asshole for doing asshole-things."

"I thought so," Malcolm said, a pinch of disappointment in his voice. "I don't know what to do. I have some ideas, but I don't know how to deal with him."

"I think you should fight back. I don't mean you should hit him, but you should start messing with him. You know, waste all of their toilet paper, put tacks on their bed, piss in their orange juice. You're good at that sort of stuff, aren't you? That's why you're here, right?"

Malcolm nodded slowly, as if he were actually considering the option. *I can't hit the old man,* he thought, *but I can mess with him.* Determination sparkled in his eyes.

He said, "I'll think about it. I don't want to hurt them, but I have to do something."

"Whatever you do, I have your back."

They closed their eyes and kissed again. Malcolm kissed her cheek, then he nibbled on her ear, then he pecked at her neck. Meanwhile, Claire kissed his cheek, forehead, and even his hair. Malcolm chuckled inwardly as he squeezed her breasts, too. He finally reached second base. The sound of lips smacking, grunting, and moaning dominated the backyard.

Five minutes passed in the blink of an eye.

Malcolm pulled away from Claire and said, "I have to go. I can't be late again."

Claire rubbed her lips together, as if she had just applied lipstick, then she said, "Okay. Listen, if you need anything from me, I live in a yellow house two blocks down the street from you. It's the same street, you just have to go left from your grandpa's house. You can't miss it. My parents don't get home till six and they're usually asleep by ten. You can come by when they're not around or when they're sleeping. Alright?"

Malcolm said, "Yeah, that sounds good. Thanks for everything. I owe you." He kissed her, then he said, "I'll see you later."

As Malcolm jogged around the corner, Claire shouted, "Text me!"

Malcolm jogged through the neighborhood, constantly glancing up at the sky. He used the sunshine to determine the time. If he checked his new phone, he feared one of his neighbors would see him and tell his grandfather. He couldn't trust anyone, so he couldn't take that risk. Fortunately, it was still sunny so he assumed he was on schedule.

He slowed his jog to a stroll as he approached his grandparents' house. He saw Ronald standing on the porch, his hands on his hips.

As he approached the porch, Malcolm asked, "Am I late, sir?"

Ronald did not respond. He stood at the top of the porch steps and stared down at his grandson. Malcolm stood at the bottom of the steps and stared up at him. He tried to keep a blank expression on his face.

Ronald asked, "How was your day, boy?"

"Good, sir."

"What did you do?"

"I went to the movies, I sat at the park, then I came home."

"That's it?"

"Yes, sir."

"That's good. That's real good. Well, you're not late so you passed the test. You should be proud of yourself, boy. Come inside and get ready for dinner. We can talk about your day some more over some meatloaf. Hurry up."

Malcolm nodded at him. He entered the house and headed upstairs. He hid his cell phone in his pillowcase, then he washed up in the bathroom while preparing his lies for the evening.

Chapter Thirteen

Sweet Dreams

Malcolm masterfully maneuvered his way through the dinner, spewing more lies than a politician seeking re-election. He washed the dishes after dinner, then he went to his room. Since his door didn't have a lock, he had to sit in front of his door in order to avoid any surprise visits from his grandparents. He spent an hour exchanging text messages with Claire—lovey-dovey messages—then he went to bed at ten.

He slept with a smile on his face, purring as he nuzzled his pillow. He saw Claire in his dream. In the dream, he was back in Los Angeles and Claire showed up at his school.

Click—the loud noise emerged in the bedroom.

Malcolm awoke, but he didn't immediately open his eyes. He could see the light through his closed eyelids. He didn't fall asleep with the light on, though.

He swallowed the lump in his throat, he released a shuddery breath, then he opened his eyes. He stared at the wall in front of him and, as expected, the lamp on the nightstand illuminated his room. He quietly counted to three, then he turned over on his bed. He cocked his head back and hopped on the mattress, startled.

Ronald, wearing a white wife beater and striped pajama pants, sat on a wooden chair beside the bed.

If he leaned forward, he could easily reach the nightstand and his grandson. The man somehow managed to look calm *and* angry, a fire burning in his eyes.

Malcolm and Ronald stared at each other for a minute. Ronald clearly had something to say, he was in the room for a reason, but he didn't utter a sound. Malcolm, on the other hand, *wished* he had something to say. The silence was killing him.

After the minute passed, Ronald smiled and said, "As you grow up, you will encounter several types of women. Some of these women will be splendid, others will be... *horrid.* Yeah, that's a good word for 'em. The good ones will be there for you through thick and thin. They'll cook for you, they'll massage your back and your feet after work, they'll keep a clean house, they'll take care of the kids, and they'll fuck you until your balls are dry. That's a good woman." He leaned back in his seat and ran his fingers through his hair, his smile warping into a frown in the process. He sighed, then he said, "The bad ones will destroy you. They'll neglect their womanly duties, they'll drain your bank accounts, they'll take your kids from you, and they'll fight with you. And, after they start those fights and *lose,* they'll play the victim. They might fuck you and they might fuck you often, but it'll only be part of the bigger scheme. They'll have your babies just to lock you down and have eighteen goddamn years of access to your money. These are the women we call sluts, bitches, whores, and cunts."

Malcolm could hear the anger in his grandfather's voice. His rant was laced with misogyny, even when he tried to compliment women. He was disgusted by his grandfather's words and terrified by his mere presence in the bedroom. So, he bit his tongue and waited for the peculiar situation to end.

Ronald continued, "Babs, your grandmother, started off as a bad one, but I turned her into a good one. I think she was still seventeen when I met her on that street corner. Yeah, it was right after I got home from the war. I gave her five dollars, then I fucked her. After that, I couldn't stop myself from going back to her. I'd go to her corner, I'd give her some cash, then I'd fuck her. I had a few scuffles with her pimp, but I taught him a lesson and he eventually learned to stay in his place."

Malcolm breathed noisily through his nose— nervous, disgusted, terrified. He didn't understand the purpose of Ronald's speech or visit. He thought: *he doesn't like most women, my grandma was a prostitute, but why is he telling me all of this?*

Staring blankly at the bed, Ronald said, "I needed healing after what I saw in Vietnam and sex happened to be the remedy. Your grandmother offered plenty of that, boy. We even 'convinced' her pimp to give us discounts for some group sessions. Chinks, wetbacks, niggers... They all joined in on the fun. Some of them were even younger than Babs. Sixteen, fifteen, fourteen... Those wild girls... Damn, those wild girls." A reminiscent smile formed on his face, as if he actually missed his deviant past. He said, "Thank God we didn't catch anything. Anyway, I eventually ran out of money. I didn't feel like paying for sex, either. So, I took Barbara and I married her. I taught her how to be a good one, but I made sure she didn't lose herself in the process. It all led to true love—and *a lot* of free sex. That's our love story, boy."

Malcolm examined his grandfather's face—his proud eyes, his arrogant smirk. He grimaced and shook his head, disgusted by the 'love' story. The tale appeared to have a happy ending, but Ronald alluded to abusing Barbara in order to turn her into a 'good' woman. He also admitted to having sex with teenagers. The story was horrific.

Ronald asked, "What's the matter? You don't like talking about girls? Is that it?"

Malcolm stuttered, "N–No, sir. It–It's just... It's nothing."

"Nothing?"

"Yeah, nothing."

"Funny. I thought this would be interesting to you. I thought you were a ladies' man, Malcolm. I really did. You're out there acting like a big shot, aren't you? You're already messing around with girls in my city, right?"

Malcolm held his breath as soon as he heard his grandfather's last question. The pieces were easy to link. *He knows about Claire,* he thought, *but how?*

Malcolm asked, "Have you been following me?"

Ronald stared at his grandson with a blank face— no emotion, *no life.* Then, he huffed and shook his head. He laughed and glanced over at the door.

He said, "Babs, get your ass in here."

Barbara smiled and nodded at the men as she entered the room. A pink silk robe covered her body, matching slippers protected her feet. Ronald beckoned to her, as if to say: *go on, start the show.*

Malcolm looked at his grandfather, then at his grandmother, incapable of understanding the bizarre situation.

Before he could say a word, Barbara started to disrobe. She smirked as she dropped the robe down to her shoulders, revealing her cleavage while sensually twisting her hips. She playfully teased the men. Then, she let the robe fall down to her feet. She shamelessly exposed herself in front of Malcolm and Ronald.

Her nude, roly-poly figure was showcased for the world to see. Her large breasts sagged over the fatty rolls of her belly—and those rolled over *other* rolls of fat. Blue and purple veins ran across her breasts, streaming away from her dark, hard nipples. The same dark veins appeared on her flabby arms and legs. Her pubic hair was straight and thick.

Malcolm sneered in disgust, closed his eyes, and lowered his head. He wasn't appalled by older people, but he certainly didn't want to see his grandmother's nude body.

Ronald kicked the mattress and said, "Open your eyes, boy. Open them or I'll gouge them out."

Malcolm whimpered upon hearing the threat. He could hear the sincerity and rage in his grandfather's voice. He already knew Ronald was willing to hurt him, too. So, he sat up in bed, crawled closer to the wall, and opened his eyes.

Ronald said, "Look at your grandmother, boy. That is an all-natural body—a God-given body. It's nothing to be ashamed of. You shouldn't be embarrassed to see her, either. She's a woman, you're a man, and you're family. That's it. That's all."

Malcolm said, "This... This isn't right. I'm not... No, I'm not supposed to see her like this."

"Like what? Nude? I just told you, boy: there's nothing wrong with this. Would it be wrong if we were nudists? Would you judge us then?"

"I... I don't know. Can you tell her to–"

"Tell her to what? To give you a little spin? Sure, boy, I can do that for you," Ronald responded. He whistled at Barbara, like a man calling his dog for dinner, then he said, "You heard him, Babs. Give him a show."

Barbara said, "Gladly."

She slowly turned around, swinging her hips left and right. Her wide ass jiggled with each step. The dimples on her butt cheeks looked deep, like bullet holes. She spread her ass and revealed her wide, gaping anus.

Malcolm grimaced and tried to look away, but he knew his grandfather would hurt him if he did. He reluctantly continued watching the show through his narrowed eyes.

Barbara completed her spin and faced Malcolm. She crouched down a bit, she spread her knees, then she ran her fingers through her pubic hair. She thrust her hips forward and spread her labia, revealing her pink vagina.

Malcolm instinctively closed his eyes and looked away again. The human body was natural, he understood that, but he refused to see his grandmother's genitalia. It was too much for him.

Ronald kicked the bed again and asked, "What did I say about closing your eyes, boy? Do you think I'm playing with you?" Malcolm opened his eyes to a squint. Ronald said, "Good, good. Now, pull your dick out and fuck your grandma."

Malcolm's eyes widened with shock. His eyes nearly bulged out from their sockets. *Fuck your grandma*—those words stunned him. He had never heard or read such a disgusting and immoral command.

He stuttered, "N–N–No. A–Are you... Are you kidding me?" He shook his head and leaned back on the wall. He sternly said, "*No*. I'm not playing this game."

Ronald said, "This ain't a game, boy. I want you to pull your dick out and I want you to fuck her."

"I'm not doing that! Stop it! Get out of my room!"

"Your room? *Your room?* This is *my* house, you stupid son of a bitch. You will do as I say or I will beat you until your red, purple, blue, and every other damn color in existence. No... You know what? If you don't pull your dick out in the next ten seconds, I'm going to castrate you. I'm going to make sure you don't pass down your pussy, faggot genes to the next generation."

Ronald pulled a switchblade out of his pocket. He snapped his wrist, which caused a four-inch blade to protrude from the handle. Malcolm's breathing intensified as he stared at the tip of the blade. He thought: *would he really do it? Is he that crazy?*

Ronald said, "One, two, three, four, five..."

Malcolm turned towards the window behind him and yelled, "Help! Help! He's–"

Ronald slapped the back of his head. Malcolm fell to his left, knocked to his side by the powerful blow. He rubbed the back of his head and glanced back at his grandfather. Before he could scream again, Ronald slapped his face. The *whack* echoed through the house and Malcolm's cheek immediately reddened.

Malcolm cried, "Stop! I'm just–"

Mid-sentence, Ronald punched Malcolm's stomach with a powerful jab. He would have hit him in the face again, but he didn't want to leave any visible bruises. The unexpected punch knocked the air out of him, though. The teenager crossed his arms over his stomach and rolled to his right, wheezing and groaning.

Rosy-cheeked, Malcolm croaked, "Okay... Okay, just stop hitting me. Please, don't hit me."

Ronald leaned back in his seat and said, "You have five seconds. One, two, three, four..."

Still wheezing, Malcolm pulled his pajama bottoms down. He covered his penis and pubic hair with his right hand.

Ronald said, "Get hard. Stroke yourself and get hard."

Tears streaming down his cheeks, Malcolm stuttered, "Pl–Please, I don't want to do this..."

"Do it or I cut it off. I'm serious, boy."

Malcolm reluctantly stroked his flaccid penis with his trembling hand. A million questions ran through his mind: *is this actually happening? This is illegal, isn't it? He can't cut it off and get away with it, right? They're molesting me, too, aren't they?* He didn't have any answers, so he refused to take any risks.

Ronald jabbed the knife at Malcolm and said, "Look at her while you do it, boy. Trust me, it'll help..."

"Oh God," Malcolm muttered.

He looked over at his grandmother. Thankfully, the tears in his eyes blurred his vision. He could still see her figure, though. Barbara grinned as she performed a little dance. She wasn't ashamed of herself, she didn't mind Ronald's abuse, she just danced.

Ronald said, "He's hard enough. He'll get harder when he's fucking you, Babs. Go ahead, sit on it."

Barbara said, "Yes, sir, big daddy."

She approached the bed. She kept one foot on the ground and placed the other on the bed. She spread her legs and labia in front of Malcolm. For a split second, Malcolm saw it all. He saw her vagina glistening in the light. He even believed he caught a whiff of it—a fishy, metallic scent.

He closed his eyes and cried, "I can't."

Ronald said, "Open your eyes or I'll chop it off. You know I'll do it, you know what I'm capable of..."

Malcolm thought: *does he know I saw the pictures in the attic?* Fearing his grandfather would actually castrate him, he opened his eyes. He tried to avoid his grandmother's crotch and breasts, so he stared at her stomach. Barbara slowly lowered herself, *inch*-by-*inch.* She squatted closer to his penis, which stood half-erect like the Leaning Tower of Pisa.

Just as the tip of his penis caressed her vagina, Barbara staggered away from the bed. She giggled and blushed as she waved one hand in front of her face. Ronald chuckled and slapped his knee, tickled. The couple looked at each other, full of joy and deviance.

Malcolm, awed by their behavior, quickly linked

the pieces: it was a joke, a sick joke. He lifted his pants up and covered himself with a blanket.

As Barbara slipped into her robe, Ronald said, "I'm glad you put your cock away, boy. It looked like you were actually going to fuck your own grandmother. For Christ's sake, that's just wrong. You Mexicans sure love that nasty shit, don't you?"

Malcolm couldn't say a word. He couldn't even tell if he was conscious, hallucinating, or dreaming. None of it made sense to him.

Ronald dragged the chair back to the desk and said, "Stop breaking the rules, boy, and everything will go smoothly for you. Keep breaking the rules... and you'll be punished. I might actually make her fuck you and, believe me, she'll do it."

Barbara smiled and said, "It would be my pleasure."

Ronald spanked her and nodded, as if to say: *get out of here.* He glanced back at Malcolm and said, "I hope you learned your lesson tonight. We do the fucking, not you. Now get some sleep. You have a lot of chores tomorrow."

Malcolm watched as his grandparents exited the room, closing the door behind them. He was dumbfounded and unnerved by the encounter.

He stared down at himself and whispered, "They're not regular 'old people.' They're not like other grandparents. No milk and cookies, no allowances, no normal stories. They're crazy. They're crazy and evil." He looked back at the door and said, "I have to fight back. I'm going to teach them a lesson..."

Chapter Fourteen

Vengeance

On Wednesday morning, Malcolm, Ronald, and Barbara shared another breakfast in the kitchen. Ronald spoke about the errands he had to run while Barbara complained about her sore feet. Malcolm remained quiet during the entire meal. No one said a word about the inappropriate encounter that occurred during the previous night. It was swept under the rug, but they all knew the mess was there.

After breakfast, Ronald tossed on a coat, he warned Malcolm about his behavior, then he departed from the house. Barbara was allowed to stay home to rest.

As Malcolm brought his plate to the sink, Barbara said, "Let me wash the dishes, hun."

Avoiding eye contact, Malcolm said, "No, it's okay. Grandpa would kill me if he saw you doing the dishes."

"Don't worry about him, sweetie. I know how to control your grandfather," Barbara responded. She rubbed Malcolm's arm with a sensual touch. She said, "Really, it's okay. I don't mind doing the dishes. You finish up your chores. I'll have some tea and cake ready for you when you're done."

Malcolm slowly pulled away from his grandmother. He didn't want to offend her with any swift or eager movements. He believed she was genuine. She would cover for him as long as he didn't insult her. *She's not like him,* he thought, *but something's definitely wrong with her.*

He nodded at her and exited the kitchen. He headed to the bathroom upstairs. He closed and locked the door behind him, then he made his way to the medicine cabinet.

He whispered, "Time for some old-fashioned revenge."

He pulled a black comb out of the cabinet and smirked. His grandfather styled his hair with that comb every morning. So, he pushed on the teeth of the comb with his thumb until they snapped off. He repeated the process four times, making it useless. He flushed the broken teeth down the toilet, then he returned the comb to its rightful place.

He said, "What's next? Come on, what's next?"

His eyes stopped on a short jar of clear hair gel. A deviant idea surfaced in his mind, a conniving smile formed on his face.

He opened the jar of gel and placed it on the sink. He looked over at the door as he unzipped his pants —*the coast was clear.* He closed his eyes and started masturbating. He thought about Claire and her breasts. He re-watched his favorite porn clips in his mind, remembering every detail of his favorite porn stars.

After two minutes of uninterrupted tugging, he opened his eyes and ejaculated in his grandfather's hair gel. He added nearly half an ounce of semen to the jar. He sneered in disgust as he mixed the gel and cum together with his index finger.

After the traces of the semen vanished and the gel looked passably normal, he washed his hands and said, "Hope you like that, you old bastard." He returned the jar to the medicine cabinet. He said, "So far, so good. What else?"

There were several prescription pill bottles in the cabinet. He spotted one that read: *Prozac.* He didn't know much about it, but it captured his attention.

As he dried his hands, he whispered, "No, I can't take it too far. He'd kill me... or maybe I'd kill him."

He decided to ignore the medicine. Instead, he grabbed a bottle of magnesium citrate—a saline laxative—then he closed the cabinet. He returned to the hall and looked down the stairs. Ronald still wasn't home and Barbara was still in the kitchen. There was still time for more vengeance.

Walking with wide strides, Malcolm eased his way into the attic. He felt his heart pounding against his ribs, he felt the beads of sweat racing down his face. He felt dizzy and nauseous, too. The blend of fear and excitement overwhelmed him. If he were caught in the attic, he feared his grandfather would torture him with his 'special' tools.

On his tiptoes, he approached the cardboard boxes in the corner. He used his cellphone to snap pictures of the grotesque Polaroid photographs depicting his grandfather's war crimes. He winced as the phone's flash illuminated the attic with each photo. He was alone in the room, but he felt as if someone were standing behind him—watching him, *haunting him.*

After photographing the last Polaroid, he sent the images to Claire. Then, he sent her a text message that read: *I'm sorry if these scare you. They're pics of my grandpa during a war. Upload 'em somewhere.*

Help me expose him. He deleted the pictures and text messages from his phone. Death was guaranteed if his grandfather found the phone and messages.

Malcolm exited the attic. The faint sound of *clinking* silverware emerged from the kitchen. He didn't hear his grandfather, though.

He whispered, "Great. I still have time."

He entered the master bedroom. He neatly made the bed with hospital corners, following his grandfather's directions to a T. While doing so, he dropped his pants to his knees and rubbed his bare ass on the pillows. He swiped the pillow cases between his butt cheeks like a credit card. It wasn't the most original form of revenge, but he didn't have many options.

After making the bed and staining the pillows with his stench, he exited the master bedroom and headed to his room. He closed the door, then he entered his closet and sat on the floor under his shirts and jackets. The next step in his plan required his voice, so he had to avoid his grandmother's ears by any means necessary.

He dialed 911 on his cell phone, then he held it up to his ear.

A female operator answered, "911, what is the nature of your emergency?"

In a soft tone, just above a whisper, Malcolm said, "Hello, I'm calling about a domestic disturbance."

"Are you in any danger right now, sir?"

"No, no. I want to report a neighbor. Every night for the past three days, I've heard a kid crying from my neighbor's house. It sounds like he's being abused and I think you should check up on him."

"Do you hear the crying now?"

"No. It's calm right now. Maybe it'll happen again tonight, but I just wanted to call now so I wouldn't forget. I'm trying to be, um... proactive."

"That's fine, sir. Can you give me your name and address?"

"The address of their house is 728 East Fur Avenue."

"Sir, I need *your* name and address. I'll file–"

"Please help him. I'm sorry, I have to go."

Malcolm disconnected from the call. He stared down at the phone, anxious and afraid. He thought: *was it enough? Will the police actually come?* He could only wait and see. He hid the phone in his pillowcase and headed downstairs.

In the kitchen, Barbara walked from cupboard-to-cupboard, preparing to serve cake and tea for a quick snack. Malcolm swept the kitchen floor, his eyes darting left-and-right as he waited for the perfect moment to strike.

As she checked the stove, Barbara said, "It's getting hot these days. I don't like the hot weather." She giggled, then she said, "If it gets any hotter, I might have to stop wearing clothes around the house. That would be something, wouldn't it?"

Malcolm gritted his teeth and nodded, as if to say: *yeah, sure, whatever.* He was infuriated by her nonchalant demeanor. She didn't touch him in the kitchen, but her words were inappropriate. She molested him during the previous night, too. He couldn't forgive her for her actions. He ignored her chitter-chatter and slunk his way to the table, still sweeping the floor.

He looked at the teacups on the table, watching as plumes of steam rose from the green tea. With his back to Barbara, the teenager pulled the bottle of magnesium citrate out of his pocket. He wrestled with his conscience as he gazed at the tea. He thought: *she deserves this, doesn't she? She's just as bad as the old man, isn't she?*

As she looked through a cupboard, Barbara said, "You know, Malcolm, you should be proud of yourself." Malcolm furrowed his brow, confused by his grandmother's statement. Barbara explained, "You have a very nice penis. It's thick and long. What is it? Six, seven inches? And that wasn't even fully erect, was it? It looks different compared to Ronald's, you must have gotten it from your real daddy, but it's cute. The girls are going to love it."

Malcolm glanced over his shoulder and scowled at his grandmother. Ronald physically and psychologically tortured him while Barbara sexually abused him. He realized something in the kitchen: *abusive guardians deserved to be punished, regardless of their age.*

He grabbed one of the teacups as he shook the bottle of magnesium citrate. The teacup was filled with nearly six ounces of tea, the warm liquid rippling close to the rim. He quietly drank nearly four ounces while his grandmother babbled about tea, cake, and penises. Then, he refilled the drink with four ounces of magnesium citrate. He shoved the bottle into his pocket and grabbed the teacup.

Malcolm turned towards Barbara and said, "Here, grandma, have some tea."

Barbara smiled and said, "Of course, honey. But,

aren't you going to join me?"

As Barbara took a sip of the tea, Malcolm said, "Not now. I should finish my chores before grandpa gets home."

Barbra frowned and smacked her lips. She said, "Well, maybe it's for the best. This doesn't taste quite right."

As Barbara turned towards the sink, Malcolm said, "Wait, um... Actually, I'll drink with you. Yeah, I'll take a sip."

He grabbed the other teacup, smiling as he tried to keep a semblance of normality. He lifted the cup, as if to say: *cheers!* His grandmother happily followed his lead. Their cups met with a *clink*, then they sipped their drinks. With that, Barbara didn't mind the odd taste of her tea anymore. She was just happy to spend time with her grandson.

A booming *thud* echoed through the house.

From the front door, Ronald shouted, "Babs, I'm home!"

Barbara took Malcolm's teacup and softly said, "Sounds like Ronnie's home. We'll have to have our little date some other time, honey. Sorry."

Malcolm responded, "It's fine. Don't worry about it."

"How was your morning, Babs?" Ronald asked from the archway.

Barbara said, "Fine. Fine and dandy."

"The boy didn't give you any problems, did he?"

"No. He worked on his chores while I relaxed with my tea."

"You sure?"

"Positive."

Ronald said, "Good. Come watch TV with me before lunch. I have to tell you about this little bastard I ran into at the bank."

Barbara followed Ronald into the living room, teacup and saucer in hand. The couple sat on the sofa and watched television. Ronald rambled about his morning while Barbara sipped her tea and listened.

Malcolm swept the kitchen, then he swept the den. Twenty minutes passed, but he didn't notice a commotion. He only heard their muffled voices and some laughter. Sweeping every step of the way, he moved back to the dining area. He constantly glanced over at the sofa as he swept the floor around the dining table.

Another ten minutes passed, then a roaring fart caused everyone to halt in the room. The volume of the television seemingly dropped by itself, the noise outside vanished in an instant.

"Oh," Barbara said, her face scrunched with worry. "I'm sorry, I don't know what–"

Ronald leaned away from her as she let out another explosive fart. Malcolm took two steps back, surprised but delighted. Barbara shook her head as she tried to stand from her seat, muttering to herself about her uncontrollable bowel movements.

Ronald asked, "You okay, Babs?"

Barbara didn't respond. She squeezed past him and hobbled towards the kitchen archway, racing to the bathroom—but it was too late. Along with another sonorous fart, diarrhea leaked out of her ass. The brownish-green liquid streamed down her vascular legs. A puddle of diarrhea formed under her feet, staining her slippers while gooey chunks of feces inflated her underwear like a diaper.

She held her hands over her mouth and cried, "Oh God..." Tears rolled down her cheeks, mucus dripped from her nostrils. She shouted, "Oh God!"

Ronald rushed to her side. He rubbed her shoulder and said, "It's okay, sweetheart, it's okay. It was just an accident. It happens to all of us."

"I–I'm sorry, Ronnie. I'm so sorry. I... I don't know what happened. I couldn't hold it."

"Hey, it's fine, Babs. Stop apologizing."

"It's not fine. I'm old, I'm sick, I'm dying. I can't believe this is happening to me."

"Don't say that, baby-girl."

Malcolm watched them with a blank expression. He looked emotionless, but he actually felt a mishmash of emotions: happiness, pity, *fear*. He didn't feel like laughing at his grandmother. As a matter of fact, he even felt some guilt in his heart. By retaliating, he felt as if he had just started a war against his grandparents.

Ronald glared at Malcolm, he pointed at him, and then he pointed at the ceiling, gesturing his demands: *go to your room.* Malcolm was happy to oblige.

Chapter Fifteen

A Domestic Disturbance

Malcolm sat on his bed, quiet and motionless. He stared at the floor and thought about the day. He tried to forget about Barbara's 'accident.' Instead, he thought about the rest of his sabotage. Specifically, he thought about his call to the police. He spent the afternoon waiting for the police to arrive, but a cop never showed up.

He muttered, "I gave them the right address, didn't I? Did they believe me? Do they even care?" He looked over at his pillow. He whispered, "Should I call them again?"

He sighed and looked at the door. His grandparents were home, so he couldn't take the risk. It was too dangerous, even if he called from the closet.

Before he could make a decision, Malcolm heard the sound of a car door slamming. He peeked out the window. A black-and-white police cruiser was parked in front of the house. He also spotted a police officer walking up to the house, the chatter from his radio disrupting the neighborhood's peaceful aura.

Malcolm smiled and said, "Perfect timing."

He crept out of his room, shoulders and heels raised. He looked down the hall. He could hear his grandmother crying in the master bedroom—she was humiliated and defeated by the prank. He felt guilty, but he couldn't forgive her for her inappropriate behavior. He slunk towards the top of the stairs, trying to avoid the creaky floorboards. He sat down on the top stair and eavesdropped.

The officer knocked on the door.

Sitting on the recliner, Ronald muted the television and said, "Who the hell is it?"

He muttered to himself until he opened the front door. He was caught off guard by the cop's presence, but he recognized him.

Officer Keith Griffin regularly patrolled the area. Middle-aged, he was a thirteen-year veteran of the police force. His hair was cut short, nearly bald, and he had a clean-shaved face. Determination and compassion sparkled in his bright blue eyes. He was a stern but caring man. He looked stronger than Ronald, too.

Griffin said, "Good evening, Mr. O'Donnell."

Ronald responded, "Good evening, Griffin. What can I do for you? Need help catching those taggers again?"

"No, sir. I'll get straight to the point. We received a complaint earlier today about a domestic disturbance."

"A domestic disturbance?" Ronald repeated quizzically.

"Yes, sir. It was a complaint of a child crying over the past three or so days. The caller accused you of abusing a child."

"Abuse? *Abuse?* No, that's a bunch of bullshit."

"Is a child staying with you?"

"A teenager. Malcolm Hernandez is staying with us. He's my daughter's bastard child."

"Okay, okay. I know you're an honest man, Mr.

O'Donnell, so I'll ask you once and only once: did you abuse him?"

Ronald huffed and shook his head, as if the man had just asked him an audacious question—*may I fuck your wife?* He controlled his anger, though.

Malcolm heard the entire conversation from the second floor. He thought about heading down and causing a scene, but he didn't want to make a fool of himself.

Ronald said, "I am a law-abiding citizen, Griffin. You and I both know that."

"I understand that, sir, but–"

"There has been no 'abuse' in this house. There has been discipline, but I know the law and I did *not* break it."

Griffin said, "I'm going to have to see the child."

"*Teenager.*"

"Excuse me?"

"He's damn-near a grown man. He's not a child."

"Either way, I need to see him. I need to conduct a brief welfare check. You know how it is."

Ronald said, "Fine. No problem." He glanced over his shoulder and shouted, "Malcolm! Malcolm, get down here! You have a visitor!"

Malcolm smiled smugly as he stood from the stairs. He didn't want to seem to eager, so he waited in the hallway for twenty seconds. He wiped the stupid grin off his face and headed downstairs.

As he approached the front door, he asked, "Who is it, grandpa?"

Ronald pulled the door open and beckoned to the officer. Griffin entered the home, his hand on his holster.

"A cop?" Malcolm said innocently, as if he didn't know about his presence.

Griffin said, "Hello, Malcolm. My name is Keith Griffin, I'm with the police department. I just want to ask you a few questions."

Malcolm shrugged and said, "Okay, sure."

"Are you okay?"

"Wha–What? What do you mean?" Malcolm asked, still playing stupid.

"Are you hurt?"

Malcolm glanced over at his grandfather, fighting the urge to smile. Ronald clenched his jaw and stared back at him, struggling to keep his composure. Griffin read the teenager's face—and he could sense his arrogance.

Malcolm said, "Yeah. I don't... I just... He's been beating me, okay? He hits me."

Griffin asked, "Do you need medical attention?"

"No, no. I'm okay right now. I mean, I'll survive, but I just want to go home. I'm sick of him and I'm sick of this place. Get me out of here. *Please.*"

Ronald said, "Like I told you, Griffin: I disciplined him, but I didn't break the law. The boy broke my rules and tried to run away, so I spanked his ass."

"That's a damn lie, man," Malcolm snapped.

"So you didn't break my rules? Is that what you're saying?"

"I'm saying I didn't try to run away."

Ronald turned his attention to Griffin. He said, "I'm a private person, I didn't want this getting out there, but I won't allow this boy to throw dirt on my name. He's not here on vacation, he's not here 'cause he loves us. He's here because he's in trouble at home. He brought a gun to school–"

"A squirt gun," Malcolm interrupted.

Ronald continued, "And he was suspended. He might get expelled and he might go to jail. That's who we're dealing with here. Don't be fooled."

Malcolm said, "None of that matters. He beat me!"

Griffin examined Malcolm's face, neck, and arms. He didn't notice any significant bruises or any other injuries.

He asked, "You mind lifting your shirt and taking a spin for me?"

Malcolm furrowed his brow. He reluctantly lifted his shirt up to his chest, then he spun in a circle. Griffin examined his body. He noticed a light red mark on his abdomen, but he didn't find any bruises or cuts. The mark wasn't conclusive, either. The teenager looked healthy, too, well-nourished and clean.

Griffin said, "You can stop." Malcolm lowered his shirt and faced the adults. Griffin said, "Mr. O'Donnell, you need to show some restraint. I understand that you believe in corporal punishment, it's your right to a certain extent, but don't push it too far. I'm not afraid to step in."

Ronald responded, "I understand. You don't have to tell me twice."

"Wait a second," Malcolm said. "You're not going to do anything about this? I told you he beats me. I'm not lying."

Griffin said, "I know, son. Your grandfather already confessed to that. It's his legal right to discipline you, though, and, as you said, you'll survive. I don't see any signs of serious injury or trauma. You look like a healthy kid. You just have to start making better decisions for yourself."

"He beat my ass with a paddle!"

Ronald huffed, then he said, "And you called *me* a liar. I don't need a paddle, a belt, a hanger, or any of that to teach you a lesson. You should be ashamed of yourself."

Griffin sensed the tension in the room. Malcolm and Ronald clearly harbored hatred for one another. He couldn't do much about it, though.

He said, "Malcolm, I understand that you're angry. I get it: you don't want to be here. But, until you go home and while you're living under his roof, you have to follow his rules. If you don't want to be disciplined, don't give him a reason. Show some respect and obey your grandfather. He's a war hero, you know? He deserves your respect. Besides, if you fly under the radar, you'll be out of here in the blink of an eye." He patted Malcolm's shoulder and said, "You can call us if you ever need anything, but, for now, there's nothing I can do."

Devastated, Malcolm watched as the officer walked onto the porch. His master plan crumbled before his very eyes, his hero walked away without saving him. Ronald leaned against the door frame and watched the officer. He was home free, but a question crept into his mind.

Ronald asked, "Who called, Griffin?"

"I wouldn't be able to tell you even if I knew. We'll get to the bottom of it if it was a prank call, though. Enjoy your night, Mr. O'Donnell."

"You too."

Griffin waved, then he left the house. He sat in his

cruiser for a moment and updated his dispatcher, then he rolled out of his parking space. With that, the confrontation ended.

Ronald closed the door, then he turned towards Malcolm—stony-faced. He said, "Go to your room."

Malcolm took a step back and asked, "You... You're not going to punish me?"

"I'll punish you, but not now. I have to try something different. I grounded you, but that didn't stop you. I spanked you, but that did *not* stop you. If I'm going to save you from yourself, I have to change my methods. Now, go to your damn room."

Malcolm couldn't read Ronald. He wanted to believe he finally scared his grandfather, but, in reality, he still feared the man. That fear flowed through his veins like acid, causing him to feel a warm sensation from head to toe. He walked backwards until he reached the staircase, his eyes glued to his grandfather, then he ran back to his room.

Chapter Sixteen

Humiliation

Despite his efforts, Malcolm couldn't literally sleep with one eye open. It simply wasn't possible. So, he lay in bed with two pillows stacked under his head and he stared out the window. He watched the street below him. He could see the porch lights across the street, a car occasionally drove past the house, but he didn't see any other cops. He felt abandoned by the world.

He nuzzled his pillow as he sniffled and whimpered. Images of his mother and Claire flashed in his mind. He remembered his friends at school and he even thought about Mr. Crawford. Guilt festered in his stomach, causing him to feel anxious and nauseous. He wished he could apologize to everyone he had wronged.

Pillow soaked in tears, Malcolm drifted out of consciousness. He didn't have the opportunity to dream, though.

His eyes flew open, wide and horrified. A putrid stench blew into his nostrils. The foul, nutty scent swallowed the room. The lamp on the nightstand was still off, but he felt a presence in the room. Someone was watching him with a set of furious eyes that pierced into his soul. He peeked over his shoulder, then he gasped and sat up straight in bed.

He saw the silhouette of a person standing towards the center of the room, barely illuminated by the moonlight.

He stuttered, "Grand–Grandpa... Grandpa, is that you?"

The mysterious person didn't move or speak. The foul stench emanated from the person, though. Without taking his eyes off the silhouette, Malcolm leaned forward and turned the knob on the lamp. He inhaled deeply as the light lit up the room.

Ronald stood in front of him, wearing his tank top and pajama pants. Black leather gloves veiled his hands. He carried a black plastic bag in his right hand. The old man stared vacantly at Malcolm. He looked as if he had mentally checked out—*absent.* A short, gooey worm of drool hung from the side of his mouth.

Speaking loudly but not quite shouting, Malcolm said, "*Grandpa.*"

Ronald said, "Today was supposed to be a simple day. I was supposed to finish my errands, Barbara was supposed to relax, and you were supposed to behave yourself. I would have given you more privileges if all went as planned. You would have earned my respect—*my love.* You couldn't behave yourself, though, could you?"

Malcolm remained quiet, stern and frightened. His eyes darted to the left. He looked at the lamp, ready to use it as a weapon at the first sign of trouble.

Ronald continued, "You called the police, didn't you? You called them while I was gone, right? How? How'd you do it, boy? Babs didn't see you use her phone and I had mine the entire time."

Don't look at the pillow, don't look at the pillow,

don't look at the damn pillow—the words echoed through Malcolm's head. He saw it in hundreds of movies: if he looked at the pillow, his grandfather would connect the pieces and find his cell phone.

Malcolm said, "I didn't call anyone. You ever think it might have been one of your neighbors? Maybe someone you punched in the past?"

"Bullshit. That is bullshit. I am going to tear this room to pieces and I'm going to find your phone while you're gone."

"Gone? What's that supposed to mean? Where am I going?"

Ronald approached the bed and said, "As you know, Barbara had a little 'accident' today. It... It really hurt her. She thinks I don't love her anymore, she thinks I'm embarrassed of her. She's downright ashamed of herself, boy. I've never actually seen her in so much pain. Never in my life. You see, I've always protected her from society's wickedness and pain—*always.* I've gotten stabbed for that woman, I've been shot at for her. So, it hurt me to see her like that 'cause I knew I failed her." He stopped next to the bed. He glared down at Malcolm and said, "I'm not supposed to fail. I know it was you, boy. You hurt my woman."

Defiant, Malcolm looked him dead in the eye and said, "You're wrong. I didn't have anything to do with that. She's just getting old. She lost control of herself. She had an accident. That's what happens to old people, right? I guess you could say: *shit happens.*"

Ronald sat on the edge of the bed. Malcolm crawled away from him, moving closer to the window. He didn't have a solid escape plan, but he had some ideas: he would either hit him with the lamp or leap out the window. The bag crinkled and rustled as Ronald reached into it. The stench rose from the bag's opening, so powerful it could be tasted.

With his fingertips, Ronald pulled Barbara's soiled underwear out of the bag. The diarrhea painted the white briefs with tints of brown, green, and even yellow. Small chunks of shit clung to the cotton, too. The feces covered most of the underwear, leaving only small patches of white. It was explosive diarrhea unlike anything they had ever seen before.

Disgusted, Malcolm said, "Put it away. I'm not going to–"

Mid-sentence, Ronald lunged at Malcolm. He grabbed the nape of his neck and stopped him from moving. Then he rubbed the soiled underwear on Malcolm's face. Malcolm gagged and coughed as he felt the cold, moist texture of the briefs on his nose, cheeks, and lips. He tried to keep his mouth closed so he wouldn't taste the shit, but he couldn't help himself. He had to scream.

Malcolm yelled, "Help! Help me! Grandma! Shit, someone–"

Ronald struck his stomach with a powerful uppercut. Malcolm crossed his arms over his abdomen and gasped, his lungs vacuumed by the blow. Ronald seized the opportunity and shoved the filthy underwear into Malcolm's mouth until his cheeks inflated. Malcolm tasted it all. It was a bitter, cheesy, and nutty flavor—*a rotten flavor.*

His taste buds were overwhelmed by the diarrhea, causing his tongue to quiver and jerk every which way. His eyes widened as he retched and shuddered. He felt a choking sensation as vomit rose in his throat like lava from an erupting volcano. His mouth was stuffed, so he couldn't vomit. He choked it down, then he tried to spit the underwear out. His eyes bulged from their sockets, thick veins protruded from his neck and brow.

Ronald grabbed a fistful of Malcolm's hair and dragged him off the bed. Malcolm slipped and slid, his bare feet gliding across the floorboards. He tried to scratch his grandfather's wrist while choking on the underwear. They nearly tumbled as they went down the stairs. Malcolm bounced from wall-to-wall like a Ping-Pong ball. The potential hazards didn't daunt Ronald, though.

Ronald dragged Malcolm down the basement stairs. He pushed his grandson into the bunker. Malcolm landed on his knees, disoriented and exhausted. He finally pulled the underwear out of his mouth and drew a deep breath.

Standing in the doorway, Ronald said, "You'll be staying in purgatory for a while, boy. Your grandmother doesn't want to see you and she doesn't want you to see her." He grabbed a water bottle—a bottle with only three ounces of water—and rolled it into the bunker. He said, "Don't waste that cleaning your mouth or your face. If you do that, you'll end up dehydrating and killing yourself in here. Good luck, boy."

Awed, Malcolm watched as his grandfather casually closed the door and sealed him in the darkness. He listened to the *clinking* and *clanking* of the locks. Once again, he was isolated and abandoned.

Eyes brimming with tears, Malcolm yelled, "Fuck!"

Chapter Seventeen

A Plan

Malcolm lay on the concrete floor, squirming and groaning. His back ached due to the hard, cold ground. The beating and the rough trip down the stairs left him sore and lethargic. His grandmother's soiled underwear, which he kicked into a corner, stained the room with a vile stench. The odor lingered in his nostrils and he swore he could taste the shit at the back of his mouth.

He felt as if he were resting in an old septic tank or a dirty sewer. He felt the bunker represented the worst living conditions. He thought about homeless people and prisoners of war: *did they have it worse?* He had shelter and he wasn't suffering from any serious injuries, but he was undoubtedly being tortured.

He muttered, "He's killing me. I'm going to die down here. Oh, shit, I don't want to die."

On his back, resting on the ground, Malcolm couldn't see the ceiling through the darkness. He tightly squeezed his eyes shut, then he opened them, but to no avail. The darkness was impenetrable. He couldn't hear anything outside of the bunker, either. He only heard his grunts, mutters, labored breathing, and heartbeat.

He had already lost track of time, but he assumed it had been hours since his grandfather dragged him into the basement. He feared it had been longer than a day. He finished his water hours ago, so he was parched. His lips, his mouth, and throat were painfully dry. For the third time since he arrived at the bunker, he considered drinking his own urine to quench his thirst. He already tasted feces, so the idea didn't frighten him very much.

He said, "I have to... to survive. I have to beat them. They... They can't get away with this. I'm going to–"

The sound of locks *clanking* seeped into the bunker. A dull *thud* quickly followed. The door slowly swung open, the hinges shrieking like a wild animal caught in a bear trap.

Malcolm struggled to his feet, his legs wobbling under him. He held his hand up and blocked the light from hitting his eyes. Through his blurred vision, he spotted his grandfather standing in the doorway.

Ronald smirked and said, "Well, I'll be damned. It looks like you actually survived. I'll be honest with you, boy: I thought I was going to have to bury you in the backyard. You know, like the cartels and their mass graves. You would have been the first, but who knows? Maybe you would have started my career as a professional killer. You call 'em 'sicarios,' right?"

Malcolm didn't respond. He breathed deeply through his nose and swayed from side to side as he glared at his grandfather. He listened to Ronald's devious laughter. That cocky cackle drove him insane.

As he recomposed himself, Ronald said, "Congratulations on your survival, boy. Really, you deserve that. But, I need you to understand something: things will get worse if you keep pushing me. I am the type to push back. And, most importantly, there are no limits to what I can do. There never have been."

Images of the war photographs flashed in Malcolm's mind. He closed his eyes and shook his head—disgusted, angry, horrified. He understood that his grandfather wasn't lying. *He doesn't have any limits,* he thought, *but that doesn't mean he can get away with this.* He realized he couldn't rely on pranks to deter his grandfather. Although he failed once already, he knew he needed the police to save him.

Changing the subject, Malcolm asked, "How long has it been? How long have I been here?"

"Twenty hours, more or less."

"What... What time is it?"

"Ten o'clock at night."

Malcolm murmured, "Ten o'clock... Okay."

Ronald beckoned to him and said, "Go upstairs. There's some food and water waiting for you in the kitchen. I want you to take a shower after you eat. We left some fresh clothes out for you. Then, go to bed. We'll start fresh tomorrow. Even-steven, okay?"

Malcolm nodded in agreement. He headed to the kitchen. He didn't see his grandmother in the house —she already went to bed—but he spotted a sandwich and a glass of water on the table. He scarfed down the sandwich and chugged the water. He still felt pain across his back and abdomen, but he was revitalized by the meal.

While his grandfather watched television in the living room, Malcolm headed to the bathroom upstairs and took a scalding shower. The water burned his skin, but it didn't bother him. In fact, he welcomed the burning sensation. He even rinsed his mouth with the hot water. He tried to clean the shit out of his mouth and nostrils, he tried to wash away the pain.

He couldn't stand it, though. He fell to his knees and sobbed, boiling water raining down on him. The sound of the shower barely masked his sorrowful cries.

After the shower, his skin was red and sensitive, and his eyes were bloodshot. He put on a fresh white t-shirt and slipped into his pajama pants.

Malcolm stared at his bedroom door, then at the master bedroom, and then at the stairs. He whispered, "I can't stay here. I need to get help. I need to stop him."

He slowly walked down the stairs. He felt like he was descending into hell, but he couldn't stop himself. He didn't have a brilliant, well-crafted escape plan. He didn't need one, either. He spotted his grandfather on the recliner as he reached the bottom of the stairs. *Don't stop,* he thought, *keep moving.* He was anxious and afraid, but he was also determined.

As Malcolm walked past the sofa, Ronald asked, "What's wrong, boy? You forget something down here?"

Malcolm didn't respond. He approached the front door.

Ronald leaned forward in his seat and said, "Hey, I'm talking to you, boy. What do you think you're doing?"

Malcolm stopped. Sweat rolled down his cheeks and neck, his heart rapidly pounded in his chest. *There's no turning back,* he thought. He rushed forward and quickly turned the locks on the door. His grandfather shouted at him, but he didn't look back. He pulled the door open and dashed out of the house, barely evading his grandfather.

Ronald stumbled onto the porch. He yelled, "Malcolm! Malcolm, get back here, son!"

Malcolm's bare feet slapped the sidewalk as he ran as fast as possible, creating a rhythmic *smacking* sound. He headed to Claire's house—his last hope.

***

"The yellow house," Malcolm said as he ran across the street. "Please be awake. I need you, Claire."

He let out a sigh of relief and slowed his run to a stroll. He approached the yellow house on the corner. In his pajamas, walking barefooted through the neighborhood, he stood out like a pedophile on a movie set—everyone could see him, but no one said a word. He easily vaulted over the picket fence. He slid on the moist grass, but he kept his footing.

He crouched and crept around the side of the house, peeking through every window in search of Claire's room. Fortunately, the house only stood one-story tall so he could see into every room. He stumbled upon the living room and a den. He even stumbled upon a bathroom, but he couldn't see much due to the frosted window.

He muttered, "Where's your damn room, Claire?"

He approached the third set of windows on the side of the house. His eyes widened as he looked through the blinds. It was a bedroom—*Claire's bedroom.*

Claire, wearing pink short-shorts and a white tank top, rested on the bed to the left. Malcolm was stunned by her effortless beauty. Her mere appearance brightened his mood and rekindled his hope.

Malcolm tapped the window with his knuckle— *clack, clack, clack.* To his utter disappointment, Claire did not awaken. So, he tapped the window faster and harder. He risked awakening her parents, but he was running out of time.

Half-asleep, Claire looked over at the window. She gasped and sat up in bed. At first glance, it looked like a pervert was watching her sleep. The mere idea made her shudder. She narrowed her eyes, then she widened them upon recognizing Malcolm.

She quietly opened the window and whispered, "What are you doing here?"

Malcolm said, "I need to talk to you. It's an emergency."

"Okay, um... Just keep your voice down, alright? My parents are sleeping down the hall and my dad has freakin' super-hearing when it comes to boys. Come on, get in here."

Malcolm climbed through the opening while Claire tiptoed to her door and turned the lock. In the small room, clothes stacked on every piece of furniture and walls decorated with posters of pop icons, Malcolm and Claire were safe from the cruelness of the cold world.

The couple sat on her bed, quiet and nervous. There was tension in the room, but it wasn't sexual or pleasant. Malcolm lowered his head and sniffled.

Tears dripped from his eyes with each blink, shuddery breaths escaped his mouth. He tried to stay silent, but he couldn't stop himself from crying.

"I'm sorry," he croaked out, trying to hide his tears.

Frowning, Claire gently rubbed his back and softly said, "It's okay, Malcolm. You didn't do anything wrong. There's... There's nothing to be embarrassed about. Talk to me. What happened? Are you hurt?"

"I did it, Claire. I messed with him like we said. I messed with their things and I even called the cops, but he... he fought back. He woke me up at night, he hit me, and he... he..."

Malcolm didn't want to tell her about the soiled underwear. It was a humiliating and disgusting experience. *He put shitty underwear in my mouth—* he trusted her, but he couldn't muster the courage to utter those words.

He grunted to clear his throat, then he whispered, "He made me taste something that... that tasted like shit. Then he dragged me into this bunker down in the basement."

"A bunker?"

"It's like a... a prison without a bed or a toilet or anything. It's just an empty room. It's purgatory, Claire, and he left me in there for twenty *fucking* hours. Goddammit, I can't beat him. I need help. Please, call the cops for me. Tell them about me, tell them about his history of abuse, tell them something. Please, Claire, I'm begging you."

Shh, shh—Claire shushed him calmly, holding her index finger over her lips. She glanced over at the door and listened to the house. It was still quiet.

She whispered, "I'm sorry, but you have to keep your voice down."

"You have to help me," Malcolm responded, his voice cracking.

"I want to help you, but... it's hard, Malcolm. I just don't know if the cops will believe us if I call them."

"You think I'm making this up?"

"No, I believe you. Your grandpa knows how the system works, though, and he's playing it like a game. Look at yourself, you don't have any bruises and you look pretty healthy. The cops need *physical* evidence to arrest Ronald, but he's hurting you on a... a psychological level. I don't know how we can prove that, though."

It was difficult to admit, but Malcolm agreed with her. Griffin, the cop who investigated his first call, didn't arrest Ronald because of the very same reasons. His track record didn't help, either. He looked like the boy who cried wolf to them—a troublemaker, *a liar.*

Claire continued, "I'm afraid. I'm afraid of everything. If I call the cops, my parents will punish me and you'll get in trouble again. And, when you leave this town, Ronald will take out all of his anger on me. I saw those pictures you sent me and... and I don't know if I can mess with him. He's scary."

Malcolm said, "This is bullshit. I have a bruise over my eye. It's fading, but it's there. My ass still hurts, too. The cop didn't ask about any of that."

"I bet Ronald told him he spanked you, right?"

Malcolm clenched his jaw and nodded—*yep.*

Claire said, "I told you: he knows the system. He'll

give them a little, but he'll get away with a lot. I've seen him do this before. It's not illegal to spank a kid and the cops probably need evidence to prove he hit you in the face, especially if he told him about your past, um... 'troubles.' He's smart, he's dangerous."

Malcolm dug his fingers into his hair and sighed in disappointment. He grimaced and tried to stop himself from bawling. Claire rubbed his shoulder, trying her best to comfort him. Her eyes welled with tears and her bottom lip quivered. The couple shared a moment of tense, depressing silence.

Malcolm whispered, "I have to do something about this. I can't go back to them."

Claire innocently suggested, "Can't you just try to follow his rules from now on?"

"No. I can't do that. I can't let him win. As soon as I got here, that old man put me in that bunker. I barely said a few words and I didn't break any of his rules. He did it just to hurt me. And you don't know all of the shit he's done to me. He's evil and he has to be stopped."

Claire nodded and said, "Okay, so... *catch him.*"

Malcolm looked over at her with a furrowed brow. He asked, "How? He's unstoppable, remember?"

"I didn't say that. I said he knows the system, so he knows how to cheat. We know the system, too. If you get evidence of him treating you like shit, they'll have to do something about it."

"But how do I get evidence?"

"Do you still have the phone I gave you?"

"Yeah, it should be in my room."

Claire responded, "Good. So, sneak into your

room right now, turn on the camera on the phone and hide it somewhere where it can record everything, and that's it. You've caught him red-handed. Give me the video and I'll upload it anonymously. He'll be all over the news just like that Judge from Texas. I remember seeing that a long time ago. It reminded me of Ronald..."

Malcolm nodded in determination. He agreed with Claire's plan, but he was still frightened. He couldn't forget about the deadly tools in his grandfather's attic.

He whispered, "Can I see your phone? I need to send my mom a text message."

Claire grabbed her phone from the nightstand and handed it to Malcolm. She said, "Go for it." As Malcolm composed a message for his mother, Claire asked, "Why don't you just call her?"

"It's late. She's always busy and she's always knocked out at night. I don't blame her, either. She's working her ass off and she's been dealing with my shit, too. I have to let her know the truth, though."

Malcolm sent a text message to his mother. The message read: *Mom, it's Malcolm. I'm sending this from a friend's phone. You have to help me. Grandpa is hurting me. I think he's going to kill me. Take me away from this place. Please take me home. I'd rather be in juvie than this hell. I'm sorry, mom. I love you.* (The lengthy message was sent as two text messages.)

Malcolm handed the phone back to Claire. He said, "If she calls or responds, tell her everything I told you. I'm going to try to catch him."

Claire kissed him, then she stroked his face, then

she kissed him again. The concern on her face was blatant. She genuinely cared about Malcolm's well-being. She was afraid of leading him in the wrong direction, too. If something happened to Malcolm because of her plan, she would never be able to forgive herself.

Claire said, "I'll do everything I can to help you. Just... Just get that evidence and let's stop this bastard."

Malcolm tightly held her hand and nodded. He felt like he was saying goodbye for the last time. He didn't want to leave his temporary safe haven, but he knew he couldn't stay forever. He kissed Claire again—one final gesture of appreciation and affection—then he climbed out the window and headed home.

Chapter Eighteen

To Catch a Monster

Malcolm climbed up the trellis on the side of the house. He moved slowly, trying to minimize the noise. The splintered wood sliced his bare feet, leaving a trail of blood in his wake, but the pain didn't faze him. The stinging pain from the puny lacerations couldn't compare to the suffering caused by Ronald's torture.

He sighed as he reached his bedroom window. To his utter relief, the room was dark and empty. He never locked the window, either, so he easily opened it with one hand. He climbed into his room, crawling onto the bed under the window. He closed the window behind him, then he glanced around the room. He looked at every dark corner, anxious.

The bed sheets were pulled off the bed, the drawers on his dresser were pulled out, and the closet was pillaged. Ronald had conducted a brief search of the bedroom. Malcolm shoved his arm into his pillowcase. His eyes widened as soon as he felt his cell phone. He thought: *the old man is vicious, but he's not as smart as he thinks he is.*

He looked at the door and whispered, "He doesn't know I'm back yet."

The clock on the nightstand read: *1:35 AM.* Malcolm tiptoed his way around the room. He grabbed a bundle of socks from a drawer on the dresser. He placed the socks on the edge of the desk, which sat parallel to his bed. He placed his phone behind the socks, aiming the camera at the bed. The socks propped up the phone while simultaneously concealing most of the device.

As he examined the setting, like a filmmaker preparing a scene, Malcolm whispered, "It's perfect. I can catch him. I can..." He shook his head and said, "No. No, something's missing. They need to see him. I need light."

He started recording on his phone. Then, with a light-footed grace, he approached the nightstand and turned on the lamp. With the light, the stage was set for a dramatic confrontation.

He stood at the center of the room and jumped five times. The floorboards creaked and groaned, and a *booming* sound echoed through the house with each jump. He used the noise as a signal—*as bait.* He wanted to capture his grandfather's attention in order to lure him to the room. The plan wouldn't work if the camera didn't catch the abuse.

Malcolm stopped jumping upon hearing a set of dull footsteps in the hallway. He heard the sound of a door opening, but he didn't hear it close. A dead silence followed the noise. Then, after thirty seconds, he heard a door *slam* down the hall.

Sweat rolling across every inch of his body, he took two steps back and stared at the door. He counted the footsteps in the hall. *He's coming,* he thought, *it's time to catch him.* He expected Ronald to enter the room with a belt or a hanger. If not, he expected a brutal pummeling from his grandfather's rock-hard fists.

The door swung open and crashed into the wall.

The door wobbled, the wall was scuffed, and the door knob became unscrewed.

Ronald stood in the doorway. Malcolm expected his angry expression so he wasn't frightened by his appearance—his scowl, his twitching nose, the rage burning in his eyes. He was, however, terrified by Ronald's weapon.

The old man tightly gripped his 'special paddle' in his right hand. The wooden paddle had a short handle, like a tennis racket. Thirteen long, rusty nails protruded from the paddle's blade. It was the paddle from the attic.

His face red with anger, Ronald shouted, "I warned you, boy!"

He marched into the room, the floorboards rattling under his feet. Malcolm was paralyzed by his fear—a deer in the headlights. He wanted to kick and scream, but he lost complete control of himself. Ronald grabbed his shirt and pulled him towards the door, causing Malcolm to stagger. He tried to drag him out of the room.

Through his gritted teeth, Ronald said, "Don't fight me, boy. I've got a little surprise for you downstairs. Get... over... *here.*"

Malcolm struck Ronald's stomach with all of his might. He couldn't knock the air out of him, but he was able to loosen his grip. He leaned back and used his weight to pull away from him. His shirt tore with a loud *shredding* sound. Ronald released his grip on his grandson's shirt, which caused Malcolm to fall to the floor.

"Damn it, boy!" Ronald barked, frustrated.

Malcolm scrambled onto his bed and, as he

reached for the window, he shouted, "Help! He's trying to kill me! Please, call the—"

Before he could open the window, Ronald grabbed Malcolm's ankle and pulled him back. Malcolm lost his balance and fell onto the mattress face-first with a *thump.* Ronald placed his left hand on the teenager's shoulder and pressed down on him, pinning his torso to the bed while his feet slid across the floor.

Ronald shouted, "This is what you get for fucking with me!"

He swung the paddle at Malcolm's ass. The long nails ripped through his pajama bottoms and penetrated his buttocks. Malcolm screamed at the top of this lungs. The shriek echoed through the house and seeped into the street.

Ronald tugged on the handle, but he encountered some resistance. Six of the nails were trapped in the boy's gluteal muscles. He pulled back until the nails *plopped* out of the puncture wounds. Blood dripped from the tip of the nails, raining down on the floorboards.

His voice raspy, Malcolm yelled, "Oh, God, help me!"

Ronald swung the paddle at his ass again. Four of the nails pierced his gluteal muscles. One nail cut into his anus. Instead of pulling it away from Malcolm's ass, Ronald pushed and pulled on the paddle, moving the nails and widening the puncture wounds. A geyser of blood squirted out of one of the wounds, painting a meter-long streak of blood on the floor.

Malcolm screamed and squirmed on the bed, but

to no avail. He couldn't escape his grandfather's grip. He felt lightheaded due to the excruciating pain emanating from his bottom.

Ronald removed the paddle from his ass. He held the paddle over his head, blood dripping on his hair, ear, and shoulder.

He yelled, "I warned you, didn't I?! I fucking warned you!"

Malcolm cried, "I–I'm sorry!"

"I guess I should have warned you in Spanish, you little prick!"

Ronald swung the paddle down at him again. He repeated the process three times: a swing, a wiggle, a removal, *repeat*. The nails easily ripped through Malcolm's pants and ass. Strips of bloody fabric spiraled to the floor, like leaves falling from trees. The rest of his pants were soaked in blood, dark and heavy.

Malcolm stopped screaming, brutalized to the point of exhaustion. He only whimpered and groaned. Parts of his shredded gluteal muscles dangled from his bottom, swaying with the torn fabric of his pants. His rear was ripped to shreds. He felt a stinging pain, but, at the same time, he felt like his ass was wiped off his body—it was gone.

Ronald stood up and said, "You dumb son of a bitch. Look at the mess you've made." As he exited the room, he shouted, "Babs! I need a towel! The boy's going to ruin this place with his blood."

Malcolm remained on the bed, astonished. He knew it happened, he could still feel the pain from his injuries, but he couldn't easily accept the abuse. His grandfather's savage methods of discipline were difficult to believe. He grimaced and panted as he wiggled on the bed. The slightest movement caused pain to surge across his entire body.

Tears dripping from his eyes, he muttered, "I can't... I can't let that bastard win. I have to... to get him back."

He fought through the pain and struggled to his feet. He walked with his legs wide apart, like a child learning to walk for the first time. He felt the warm blood dripping from his mutilated ass, he heard the blood *plopping* on the floorboards. He leaned forward on the desk and grabbed the phone. It was still recording.

He stopped the recording and said, "I've got him."

His fingers trembled as he frantically tapped the screen. He tried to attach the video to a text message, but the file was too large. He opened the Twitter app, hoping to upload the video, but he couldn't type his username and password because of his shaky fingers.

He cried, "Damn it, damn it, damn it..."

He gasped upon hearing footsteps in the hall. He lurched over to the dresser, slipping on his own blood. He pushed the dresser in front of the door, blocking half of the doorway. The effort aggravated the wounds on his ass.

From the hall, Ronald realized Malcolm was trying to barricade the door. He heard the screeching of the floorboards. He threw the towel over his shoulder, then he rammed the door with his entire body.

He shouted, "Open this damn door, boy!"

Malcolm crawled away from the dresser. He

couldn't upload the video, so he dialed his mother's number instead. He held the phone up to his ear, his hand trembling uncontrollably as he glanced over at the door. His grandfather's shouts resembled a monster's roar—deep, loud, *evil.*

"Pick up. Pick up. Please pick up," Malcolm whispered as he listened to the tone.

He cried as his grandfather's burly arm squeezed through the gap on the door—he was almost in the room. Over Ronald's growling and barking, he heard his mother's voicemail message.

Frantic with fear, he shouted, "Mom, he's going to kill me! You have to get help! Please, mom, I'm sorry for everything! Get me out–"

Ronald plucked the phone out of his hand. He threw the phone at the wall and it shattered upon impact. The screen cracked, the plastic lid snapped, and the battery fell out. Malcolm was awed. His only lifeline was destroyed before his very eyes. He couldn't tell if his message reached his mother, either.

Malcolm looked up at his grandfather and stuttered, "You–You–You can–can't do this. You–"

Mid-sentence, Ronald kicked Malcolm's face with his bare foot. Malcolm fell to his side, dazed by the blow. Ronald lifted his foot over the teenager's head, then he stomped on him. His heel struck his jaw and knocked him unconscious. Malcolm's head rolled on the ground as he snorted and groaned.

Ronald muttered, "Look at what you made me do..."

Chapter Nineteen

Your New Home

Malcolm gasped as he awoke, sweat trickling down every inch of his body. He couldn't see a thing in the room, but he recognized the thick darkness—*the bunker*. He tried to move, jerking left and right, but he was trapped. He realized that he was locked into the wooden pillory from the attic, his head and hands secured in the holes. And the pillory was bolted to the ground.

The short height of the pillory's horizontal post forced him to stand on his knees on the concrete, which caused waves of pain to surge across his legs. The post's height was adjustable, so he was purposely forced to stand on his knees. It was a calculated method of passive torture. He couldn't stand, he couldn't twist his legs, so he could not relieve the pain on his knees.

Malcolm cried, "No, man, no! This can't be happening! This is sick, damn it! It's sick! No, no, no... Just... Let me out, man! Let me out!"

He thrust his hips forward and stared down at himself. Through his tears and the darkness, he could see his body. He was stripped down to his boxers. The underwear was clean and fresh, so someone changed him while he was unconscious. His ass still stung due to the vicious paddling, but he felt some bandages clinging to his rear.

He whispered, "How long was I out?"

He looked in every direction, searching for a clue. Slowly but surely, his fragmented memory started to fall into place. A blurred memory played in his head, like a low-resolution video. After the beating, his grandfather dragged him down the hall while his grandmother followed them. He could still hear Barbara's gentle humming. She looked peaceful and happy, a tight-lipped smile on her face.

Malcolm said, "They're going to kill me. I'm going to die down here..."

He sighed and closed his eyes as light illuminated the room from the ceiling. The light blinded him for a moment. He rapidly blinked, trying to adjust to the sudden change. He heard the sound of locks *clanking* on the other side of the door.

"Shit," he whispered. "They–They're coming in. They've got me."

The hinges squealed as the door swung open. Malcolm looked up and whined. Through his blurred vision, he could see Ronald standing in the doorway. Barbara stood behind the old man, curious but cautious.

Ronald said, "You're awake. Good, good. Now we can get down to business."

Ronald and Barbara entered the room. Ronald's boots clicked on the floor with each slow step— click, click, *click*. Barbara shuffled into the room in her slippers, barely lifting her feet as she moved. She stood near the doorway, fingers interlocked over her belly. Ronald stopped in front of his grandson, staring down at him with a hateful gaze.

Malcolm sniffled and panted, unable to say a word. Even if he could speak, he didn't know what he would say. *I'm sorry?*—he was beaten and pilloried in a dungeon-like bunker, so he figured it was too late for apologies.

Ronald said, "I'll get straight to the point. You'll be spending the rest of your days in this bunker. And, in this bunker, I'm going to attempt to cure you. I'm going to cleanse you of your bad genes. That crooked Aztec warrior you hold within, he's dying here. He'll be replaced with an honorable man—*a true lionheart.* You'll mature into a respectable adult under our watch." He extended his arms away from his body and looked at each corner of the room. He said, "This... *this* is drastic, but these are necessary measures. It's just like 'Nam, boy. Sometimes you have to destroy a village in order to save it... Sometimes you have to destroy a man in order to rebuild him."

Malcolm said, "I–I'm hurt. I–I need to... to see a doctor."

"A doctor? Are you kidding me? We haven't even gotten started yet, boy. All of the things we've done to each other in the past, those are bygones. We're starting fresh."

"If we're starting fresh, then... then there's no reason for you to hurt me. You can let me go, right?"

Ronald stared at Malcolm with a deadpan expression. He didn't look angry or amused. Then, after fifteen seconds of dreadful silence, he cracked a smile.

He said, "You still have that smart mouth on you, huh?"

Malcolm shook his head and said, "No, I'm sorry. I didn't mean it like that. I was just–"

"Let me tell you what's going to happen down here," Ronald interrupted. "The laws of American society, the laws of humanity... They don't exist down here. This is like... like... like Mexico, the land of no law. You like Mexico, don't you?"

Malcolm lowered his head and mumbled, "I've never even been to Mexico..."

Ronald continued, "In this bunker, I'm going to push you beyond your limit. I will do 'things' to you that society wouldn't normally accept, especially modern society. No, boy, this ain't a place for pussies. This is hell for people like you."

Purgatory, hell, Malcolm thought, *what's the difference?* He was tired of arguing, though, so he bit his tongue. He looked over at his grandmother with sad, droopy eyes. Barbara remained quiet. She didn't interrupt her husband, she wasn't concerned about Malcolm's health.

As he walked around the pillory, like a buzzard circling its prey, Ronald said, "If I had put your father in this position before you were born, I'm convinced I could have made him into a real man. He would have stuck around and he would have raised you right. None of this would be happening if your father didn't run off. Hell, it wouldn't be happening if Jen just stayed away from those wetbacks. I tried to warn her. I really did."

"We did our best, Ronnie," Barbara said, chiming in. "At least Jenny turned her life around after he left."

"She couldn't raise her son, though. She failed miserably and we both know that."

"He's a bad one, but he's not the worst. He can

still be saved from himself. You can do it. I know you can change–"

"This is wrong," Malcolm interrupted, his voice cracking with fear. He looked up at his grandparents and said, "People will be looking for me. I have friends and... and family. My mom will ask questions. I have people talking to her right now, telling her everything. They'll lead her here and she'll bring the police."

Ronald took a knee in front of Malcolm, lowering himself to his eye-level. He said, *"Claire.* You're talking about Claire, aren't you?" Malcolm clenched his jaw and held his breath. Ronald smiled and said, "Yeah, I know all about that girl. *Claire Olson.* I've been good friends with her father for years. Unfortunately, Claire won't be able to help you. You see, early this morning, before the sun rose, 'someone' broke into her room and shot her. 'Popped in the head with an old revolver,' they said. She's dead and gone, boy."

A single tear rolling down his cheek, Malcolm stuttered, "N–No. You–You're lying."

"It's for the better anyway. Think about it, boy. You remember when you first got here? Those first two days? You were a well-behaved kid. Shit, you were a decent kid. Then, you went out and met that girl and you couldn't control yourself around her. She poisoned your brain and you started acting up. She set you up to fail. I told you: women can bring out the best in men... and the worst."

Malcolm's bottom lip quivered as he thought about Ronald's claim. *Popped in the head with an old revolver*—he remembered the revolver he found in his grandfather's nightstand. He thought: *did he really kill her?*

Saliva spurting from his mouth, he shouted, "Damn it! Why are you doing this to me? To us?! We're just kids!"

Malcolm lowered his head and screamed at the top of his lungs. He released all of his rage in a blurt of noise—*ahh!* Veins bulged from his arms, neck, and brow while his skin reddened. His screaming even caused pain to surge from his mutilated ass.

Ronald rubbed his right ear as he stood up. He said, "That's the first thing we're going to fix: your goddamn screaming. I can't stand that. Men don't scream at other men. So, to fix that, we're going to leave you in here until you've learned to watch your mouth. Maximum solitude. Enjoy it, boy."

"No, no, no. Please don't leave me in here. Let me go," Malcolm pleaded. Ronald led Barbara out of the room, then he closed and locked the door. Malcolm shouted, "No! I'm sorry! Please let me out! I'll do anything! I'll–"

Mid-sentence, the light in the bunker went out. The pitch-black darkness quickly swallowed Malcolm. Silence smothered the room. The abused teenager was abandoned in the bunker, pilloried and left alone with his sorrow.

Chapter Twenty

Solitude

In a dark void of space, isolated from civilization, it was difficult to keep track of time. A minute could be mistaken for five, an hour could feel like a day. To social beings like humans, solitude was also harmful. Complete isolation had terrifying effects on the human mind, warping one's perception of reality.

During his first hour in the bunker, Malcolm yelled at the top of his lungs. He shouted different variations of the same thing: *help! I'm in the basement! I need a doctor! Grandpa! Grandma!* His grandparents didn't acknowledge him. The neighbors didn't notice his yells or his absence. Yet, he still screamed, yelling until his throat stung and his voice broke.

He spent the second hour trying to shift the pain away from his aching knees. His weight pushed his bare knees down to the concrete, which caused insufferable pain to spread across his shin and thighs. He found some relief by lifting his knees off the ground and standing on his tiptoes, but he couldn't hold that position for longer than three minutes at a time.

As soon as he dropped down to his knees again, the pain returned. In fact, it felt much worse. He felt like his knees were broken. He couldn't move without restarting the pain.

Malcolm whimpered and mumbled to himself as he glanced around the bunker. From the corner of his eye, it looked as if the darkness were moving, like a bank of fog in the morning. However, whenever he looked at it, the darkness would stop moving. He couldn't help but wonder if he was hallucinating.

During the third hour, the imprisoned teenager stared down at his body and cried. He didn't cry because of the bleak situation, though. He sobbed because he couldn't control his bodily functions. He tried to hold it in, but to no avail.

First, he pissed himself. The tawny urine soaked his boxers and streamed down his legs. A puddle of warm urine formed under his knees. Then, he defecated himself. The wounds on his buttocks and anus stung as feces filled his boxers. The heavy crap pulled his boxers down an inch. A piece of shit even rolled out of his boxers and splashed in the puddle of piss.

He was humiliated by the 'accident,' rosy-cheeked and teary-eyed, but it still felt oddly appropriate. *Karma,* he thought, *I'm sorry, grandma.*

Malcolm dozed in and out of consciousness. It was difficult to sleep in a pillory, though. His head was locked into place at the neck. So, while he slept, he inadvertently placed pressure on his throat and choked himself. He could only sleep for a few minutes, then he would wake up, out of breath and disoriented. With very few options on the table, he continued the process for a few hours—sleep, wake up and breathe, *repeat.*

Malcolm awoke as the bulb above him

illuminated the bunker. He heard the sound of locks clanking on the other side of the door. With heavy-lidded eyes, he glanced over at the doorway. Barbara pushed the door open with a swing of her hips. She carried a plastic tray of food in her hands with a bundle of towels tucked between her arm and rib cage. Her hands were veiled with yellow rubber gloves.

She swayed her head and, in a soft voice, she said, "Go on, get in there."

Malcolm furrowed his brow as a wet, dirty rat scurried into the room. He thought: *why is she bringing that rat in here?* He couldn't muster the courage or energy to confront her about it, though.

As she walked into the bunker, Barbara said, "Pee-yew, it stinks in here."

She stopped in front of the boy and stared down at the puddle of piss. Her nose wrinkled upon catching a whiff of the feces.

She pouted and said, "You had a little accident. That's okay. Babs will clean this mess and make you feel better. Don't worry about a thing, baby."

Malcolm cried hysterically, snot bubbles popping under his nose and saliva dripping from the side of his mouth. The physical pain, the isolation, and the embarrassment devastated him.

Barbara placed the tray on the ground and slowly fell to her knees—one knee at a time. She used one of the towels to mop the urine, then she used a different towel to dry the floor. She tugged on the waistband of Malcolm's boxers, shaking his underwear until all of the clumps of shit fell to the floor. She wrapped the feces in one of the wet towels.

As she pushed the towels to one side, Barbara asked, "Would you like me to... to wipe you?"

"N–No, I–I don't think so."

"Are you sure? If I don't clean you, you might get an infection. You have cuts, remember?"

"I don't... I don't know."

"Don't worry. I'll be gentle. Just remember: I expect *you* to be cleaning *me* someday."

Barbara grabbed a small towel from the bundle. She shoved the towel into his underwear. Malcolm hissed in pain as she wiped his ass. She threw that towel aside, then she grabbed another small towel.

She said, "We have to dry your other 'parts,' too."

"No, it's–"

Barbara didn't take 'no' for an answer. She shoved the towel into his underwear and caressed his genitals. She rubbed his penis and fondled his scrotum. Malcolm closed his eyes and looked away, shocked and disgusted. He couldn't move away, though. Fifteen seconds, thirty seconds, forty-five seconds, *a minute*—she stopped touching him after a minute elapsed.

Barbara threw the towel at the stack and said, "There. You're all clean." She turned towards the food tray, then she stopped. Smirking, she glanced over at Malcolm and whispered, "It's okay. I won't tell your grandfather about your 'stiffy.' It'll be our little secret. Or maybe it's a big one..."

Malcolm groaned while his grandmother giggled. He was appalled by her perverted actions, but he couldn't attack her—physically or verbally. He planned on using her to escape from the bunker. He looked over at the food. He recognized the meal: stale chicken soup and a glass of water.

Barbara fished a piece of chicken out of the bowl with a spork. She led the spoon to Malcolm's mouth, as if she were feeding a baby. Malcolm reluctantly accepted the food. The liquid was sour and cold while the chicken was chewy.

As he chewed, Malcolm said, "Grandma, I'm sorry for everything. Grandpa was right. I put that laxative in your tea, I'm the reason you had your 'accident.' I'm so sorry." Barbara, ignoring the apology, shoved another spoonful into his mouth. Speaking with his mouth full, Malcolm said, "I'm... serious. I learned my... lesson, okay? Can you let me go? Please? I'll do anything, grandma. *Anything.*"

Another spoonful of soup went into his mouth. He grimaced in disgust, but he was able to choke it down.

Barbara said, "I'm here because Ronnie allowed me to visit you. He wants me to keep you alive and strong. Believe me, he doesn't want to kill you. He may not show it like other men, but he loves you."

Malcolm raised his brow and cocked his head to the side. *Love,* he thought, *that man doesn't know real love.* He accepted another piece of chicken.

Barbara continued, "I personally wouldn't feed you this garbage, sweetie, but it's part of his master plan. It's part of his... his 'itinerary of discipline,' I think he called it. It's going to help you grow into a mature adult. But, you also have to eat if you want to grow up big and strong. Come on now, finish up."

Malcolm didn't agree with his grandparents. Discipline—or more accurately, *abuse*—wasn't going to help him grow. He agreed with his grandmother's last statement, though: if he wanted to survive, he had to eat. So, he ate the rest of the rotten meal. Then, his grandmother slowly dumped twelve ounces of water into his mouth. The soup made him gag and retch while the water reinvigorated him.

As Barbara cleaned up, piling the towels on the tray, Malcolm said, "Please, grandma, help me get out of here. I'm begging you." His grandmother grabbed the tray and headed for the exit. Malcolm said, "Please, Grandma Babs, I... I love you. Don't you love me, too?"

Barbara stopped outside of the bunker. She glanced back at Malcolm and said, "Ronnie will be here soon. He's going to teach you a few lessons. Stay strong and I might reward you later."

Barbara licked her wrinkly lips and winked at Malcolm, then she closed the door and turned off the light. Malcolm was speechless. He was disgusted by Barbara's inappropriate behavior and horrified by the imminent abuse. He thought: *oh, shit, what's next?*

Chapter Twenty-One

The First Step to Manhood

Two hours had passed since Barbara visited the bunker, but it felt like two days to Malcolm—two long, dreadful days. The sharp pain in the teenager's knees increased with each passing hour. His stomach cramped and vomit clogged his throat because of the expired food. He was hurt and sick, so a cold sweat drenched every inch of his body.

A wave of light poured into the bunker as the door swung open. Then, with a clicking sound, the bulb in the bunker emitted a mustard-yellow glow.

Malcolm squinted as he glanced over at the door. The sudden change from dark-to-light, and vice versa, caused his head to hurt. He saw the figure in the doorway, though.

As he walked into the room, Ronald said, "I hope I didn't keep you waiting. I had to make some preparations. This sort of... *project* takes time, patience, and persistence." He dropped a duffel bag in front of the pillory. He pointed at the bag and asked, "You see that? That's your first step to manhood right there, boy, and the first step is always the hardest. If you get through this, I think you'll be able to get through anything."

Staring down at the bag, Malcolm thought: *get through what? What's in there?* He deciphered Ronald's language. 'Project' meant 'torture' and 'get through' translated to 'live through.' Pain seemed to be inevitable.

Malcolm said, "Grandpa... You won't get away with this. You can't just... just hurt someone without any consequences. If you let me go, I promise I won't tell anyone. I won't tell my mom, the cops... *anyone.* The only way you'll actually get away with this is if you let me go now, if you take this deal. It's... It's not too late."

"Begging, bargaining, bitching... You see, that just proves to me that you're not a man. It shows that you haven't learned shit since your whore of a mother dropped you off here. It's pathetic."

"Don't do this..."

Ronald crouched down to Malcolm's eye level. He said, "I'll do as I please. And I'm not 'getting away' with anything because I'm not doing anything wrong. Remember, this room isn't part of that pussy-filled world up there. And, when you eventually leave this room—*if* you leave this room—you will cooperate and follow my every order, just like a good soldier. I will break you down here, boy, and I will make you into a man."

Malcolm tried to keep a straight face, but he couldn't fight off his emotions. He sobbed intensely, wheezing and groaning. He cried until he was out of breath, his face as red as an apple. Ronald sneered in disgust, sickened by his grandson's frailty. Malcolm had the O'Donnell genes in him, but he was a failure in Ronald's eyes.

Malcolm said, "Please, I just... I want to see my mom. I want to go home. I don't... Shit, man... I mean, sir, I don't want to be here anymore. You win, okay? Just let me go home already. Let me see my mom."

Ronald clicked his tongue, then he said, "Well, you won't be seeing her until we're done here. I'll tell you something, though. Your mother, Jenny, she's been worried sick about you and she's been looking for you. She thinks I hurt you. You believe that? Where the hell did she come up with such a crazy idea?"

Malcolm's eyes widened with hope, but he quickly looked away from his grandfather. He didn't want Ronald to notice his optimism. He thought: *she got my messages, mom is on the way to save me.*

Ronald continued, "But it doesn't matter. Not one bit. You see, you share something with your mother: her cowardliness. So, she refuses to come to this house. She sent a police officer to my house today, but, fortunately for me, I called the cops last night and told 'em you ran away."

"No," Malcolm said in an awe-inspired voice.

"*Yes.* That cop your mom sent, he just made me fill out some report. That's all. Now, I just have to convince them that you actually ran away. That shouldn't be too hard, either. You remember when Griffin came by, right? That cop they sent last time you called?"

Malcolm slowly nodded. He remembered Griffin. The cop refused to help him because of a lack of adequate evidence.

Ronald asked, "You remember what I told him, don't you? I told him you tried to run away, remember?" He chuckled, then he said, "So, Griffin already knows you have a history of disappearing. He'll cover for me and he won't even know it. It's funny how things work out, isn't it?"

Malcolm responded, "They won't believe you. Just look at me. I have cuts all over my ass, you're feeding me rotten food, *I'm sick.* I'm already injured and, if you keep going, no one will ever believe your lies! No one! I mean, what the hell are you going to tell them? I fell off a mountain? I got my ass *literally* kicked by some guy with spiked boots? This isn't going to work, grandpa. Just let me go."

"It will work because, after I'm done with you, you will do anything I say. You will confess to running away, to being jumped by a pack of thugs, then returning to the house of 'good old grandpa' and collapsing on the porch. That's what's going to happen. End of story."

Malcolm heard the anger and determination in his grandfather's voice. He was surprised by the old man's unwavering desire to abuse him. It was like a hidden fetish to him—deviance disguised as discipline.

Ronald said, "Let's begin."

***

Ronald turned a crank handle on the side of the pillory. The horizontal post of the pillory rose an inch with each crank of the handle, slowly pulling Malcolm up to his feet. Malcolm's knee pain was relieved, replaced with a numb sensation. His legs wobbled and his ankles ached, though. The post stopped rising, leaving Malcolm on his tiptoes. He had to try to stand or else he would suffocate due to the wood of the pillory around his neck.

Malcolm stuttered, "Wha–What are you going to do to me?"

Ronald did not respond, quiet and emotionless.

He pulled a short, rigid wooden paddle out of the duffel bag. Without warning, he swung the paddle at Malcolm's right leg. Along with Malcolm's shriek, a loud *thud* echoed through the basement with the hit. He pulled the paddle back, then he swung it at the same leg. He struck his aching kneecap—it wasn't numb anymore. The *thud* of the blow was accompanied by a hair-raising *crunching* sound. His kneecap shattered.

As he tried to move his legs back, Malcolm shouted, "Stop! Stop! Stop!"

Stop—the word didn't exist in Ronald's vocabulary. He certainly wasn't going to take orders from a child, either.

The old man gritted his teeth and swung down at Malcolm's knee again. A deep, wide gash formed on his kneecap. Blood bubbled out of the laceration and streamed down his shin. He struck it once more, blood dripping from the paddle as he brought it back over his shoulder. The gash stretched and widened with the blow. His broken bones and ligaments could be seen through the gushing blood.

Malcolm breathed throatily as he looked every which way. The pain sent him into a delirious state. He couldn't believe the situation.

Ronald roared as he swung the paddle at Malcolm's right shin—one, two, three, four, *five times.* Each strike was accompanied by a spine-chilling *thud,* hollow and loud. Malcolm's right tibia was cracked and the skin on his shin was lacerated. His right leg, rivers of blood flowing across it, trembled violently. His foot constantly tapped the concrete floor.

As he examined the damage, Ronald said, "You always break one leg to stop your prisoner from escaping. There's no point in breaking both, but... that option is still on the table. Be grateful for the time being."

Between his heavy, raspy breaths, Malcolm said, "You... You didn't... You didn't have to do that." He tightly squeezed his eyes shut and hissed in pain. He choked down the lump in his throat, then he said, "My legs... My legs were already hurting before you got here. It's the... the concrete. You didn't have to break it. Oh, God, it fucking hurts so much."

"That's the point. It's only going to get worse when I drop you down again."

Disregarding his grandson's cries, Ronald knelt down and riffled through his supplies. The bag was clearly filled with tools of torture. He grinned as he pulled out a homemade cat-o-nine-tails. The whip had a handle made out of PVC piping. Nine strips from a rubber tire were attached to the handle. The strips were fifteen inches long.

He wagged the whip at Malcolm and said, "The Vietcong were a poor but brutal adversary. They used something like this to torture their prisoners of war. They whipped 'em until they were covered in blood from head-to-toe, until pieces of their skin hung from their bodies like string cheese. Let's see how you handle it."

As his grandfather walked around him, Malcolm said, "No, wait. Please, grandpa, I'm begging you. I said I was sorry. I'm ready to be a man. Don't do this!"

Ronald stood behind him. He swung the whip at

the air a few times—*whoosh, whoosh, whoosh.* He practiced his swing while terrifying his grandson with the noise.

Malcolm cried, "Please, don't do it. I want to–"

Ronald swung the whip with all of his might, lashing Malcolm's back. The rubber strips left seven rosy marks across his skin. Red-faced, Malcolm screamed and shook on the pillory. He felt a burning sensation on his back.

Ronald swung the whip at him again—*crack!* The rubber tails broke his skin, leaving three thin lacerations on his back. Blood dripped from the wounds, rolling down to his underwear like beads of sweat after a race.

Malcolm screamed, then, out of breath, he croaked, "Please... stop. It... It... It hurts. Please, grand–"

Malcolm yelped as Ronald whipped him again. Four more cuts formed on his back. Blood dripped from the tails, plopping on the ground like water from a leaky faucet. Ronald whipped him again and again, focusing his effort on the teenager's lower back. The rubber tails glistened with blood and wavered like snakes.

Malcolm writhed in agony as he screamed. He could hear his skin *ripping* with each strike. He couldn't know for certain, but he felt like there were at least two dozen cuts across his entire back. He also felt part of his latissimus dorsi muscle dangling *away* from his body. The sinewy muscle twitched and pulsated.

Blood covered nearly every inch of his muscular back, cascading over the other gashes and streaming down to his underwear.

He clenched his fists and stood on his only good leg, trying his best to stand. *I can survive,* he thought, *I can't bleed to death, I can't suffocate.*

Ronald shoved the whip into the bag. As he prepared for the next round of torture, he asked, "You still with me, boy?"

Dazed and exhausted, Malcolm stuttered, "You–You can't... do this. You... You can't..."

"We already went through that. Since you're still talking, I'm guessing you're good for another round. I must admit, boy: I'm impressed. I expected to have you unconscious with the broken leg, but you're still awake. Good for you, boy, good for you."

"Don't do this..."

Ronald stood up and lifted his hands up to his head, his palms facing his body. He wore brown gloves made out of cotton duck fabric and leather— durable and comfortable. The glove on his left hand was normal while the other glove was modified. Dozens of shards of glass—some small, some large —were super-glued to the knuckles of his right-hand glove. The fragments sparkled with the light.

Ronald said, "You're a strong kid. I can see that in your figure. I bet you wooed that girl with those lean arms, huh? You probably tried to seduce your grandmother with those abs, too, didn't you?"

His voice breaking, Malcolm cried, "No, I didn't... Why are you doing this, man?"

"Don't lie to me, boy. Babs told me about her visit. You made her fondle your cock, didn't you?"

"No! She's lying! She touched me! She molested me!"

"You stupid boy," Ronald said. As he swung at him, Ronald shouted, "Stop lying to me!"

The old man hit Malcolm with a right hook. The punch landed on the left side of his torso. Malcolm closed his eyes and coughed. The air was sucked out of his lungs with the blow. Six jagged cuts formed on his abs. Some shards of glass dislodged from the glove and became trapped in the cuts.

Malcolm mumbled, "S–Stop, please..."

Ronald grabbed a fistful of Malcolm's hair. He hit the boy with a powerful uppercut. The punch landed on the center of his abdomen, creating a small but deep gash. One of the larger shards protruded from the cut.

Uppercutting him between every word, Ronald said, "Learn... your... goddamn... place!"

He switched his strategy and hit him with hooks, pounding his ribs until the bones cracked. The thin cuts didn't bleed as much as the thick gashes, but all of the wounds still stung. Warm rivers of crimson blood rolled down his abs.

Malcolm panted, devastated by the abuse. Each breath aggravated his broken ribs. Pain flowed down to his broken leg from his lacerated torso— and then the other way around.

Ronald grabbed a fistful of Malcolm's hair with his right hand and lifted his head up. Some shards of glass fell into his wavy locks.

The old man swung at Malcolm's head with his left hand. He *pounded* the right side of his face with a flurry of powerful hooks. Malcolm's face immediately reddened. Blood oozed out of his nostrils and a cut formed across the side of his mouth. A gash stretched across his cheekbone, wide and bloody. Then, his left eye swelled up.

Yet, even after the final blow, Malcolm still remained conscious. He was dazed and tired, but he was still awake. He was a fighter.

Ronald removed his gloves—right first, then the left. He threw the gloves into the bag and sighed. He wouldn't admit it, but discipline was an exhausting business. He wasn't a young man anymore. He turned the crank and lowered the horizontal post until Malcolm stood on his knees again. Then he grabbed the duffel bag and walked to the doorway.

He looked back at Malcolm and said, "Your grandmother will be here soon, boy. She'll take care of you."

Malcolm did not respond. He listened to the sound of the door closing as he stared down at the filthy rat in the bunker. The rat appeared to be consuming the blood splattered on the floor. He thought: *I might have to eat that rat or myself to survive if I don't get out of here soon.* The mere possibility terrified him. The light went out and darkness swallowed the room.

Chapter Twenty-Two

Intermission

The light flickered on and off until it steadily illuminated the bunker, forcing the shadows to find refuge in the corners of the room. The sound of locks *clicking* and *clanking* followed, then the door swung open.

Barbara took one step into the bunker, then she stopped. Her eyes and mouth widened with shock. Streaks of blood stained the floor around the pillory. A few droplets of blood even stained the ceiling. Only the sound of raspy breathing echoed through the basement.

Upon noticing the light, Malcolm lifted his head and gazed at his grandmother. He was still stunned by the violent abuse. He found some relief in his grandmother's presence, though. *It didn't take her long,* he thought, *was it a few minutes or did I fall asleep?*

Barbara held a tray of food in her hands while clenching another bundle of towels between her bicep and her rib cage. A red bag with a white cross on the side was slung over her shoulder—a first-aid kit.

Without taking her eyes off her grandson, she turned her head to the side and whispered, "Come on, come on. Get in there, boy."

Malcolm furrowed his brow as he spotted another dirty rat running into the bunker. The rats concerned him, but his injuries were far more worrisome.

Barbara placed the tray on the floor in front of the pillory. She unzipped the first-aid kit and said, "I'm going to patch you up first, then I'll feed you. Okay, baby?"

Malcolm nodded—*okay.*

Barbara pulled a pack of antiseptic wipes out of the bag and said, "This is going to sting."

Barbara tugged on his right thigh and forced him to raise his leg, like a dog peeing on a bush. Malcolm gasped as Barbara dabbed the antiseptic wipe against the wound on his broken kneecap. She used another wipe to clean the cut on his shin. Then, she neatly wrapped a gauze bandage over his kneecap and shin. She couldn't fix his broken bones, but she did relieve some of his pain.

Barbara slid a folded towel under Malcolm's right leg, then she helped him slowly lower his knee. The towel reduced the pain in his busted kneecap.

She said, "There you go. Now let's clean up your back."

Barbara pushed the first-aid kit to the other side of the pillory. She stood on her knees behind Malcolm, awed by his injuries. At the same time, she couldn't help but smile. His muscles, bloody and mutilated, made her mouth water. She dumped water on his back, causing him to wince and tremble, then she cleaned his back with a towel. The towel under his knee absorbed some of the bloody water, too.

Barbara said, "I'm going to disinfect these, okay? Stay calm."

Malcolm croaked, "O–Okay..."

He hissed and groaned as his wounds were disinfected. Yet, he still appreciated his grandmother's aid. He didn't have the opportunity to thank her, though.

On her knees, Barbara shuffled her way to the front of the pillory. She leered at his defined, bloody abs. With a trembling hand, she pulled a pair of tweezers out of the bag.

Still hypnotized by his body, she stuttered, "I–I have to... to get this glass out. This is going to hurt."

She grabbed one of the shards of glass in Malcolm's wound with the tweezers. She accidentally wiggled the shard because of her trembling hand, unwittingly aggravating the cut. Malcolm screamed at the top of his lungs as the cut was widened by the tweezers. Blood squirted from the wound. He twisted his hips and tried to pull away from his grandmother.

Barbara said, "Oh, don't be such a baby. Stay still or you're going to hurt yourself."

Malcolm continued to whimper and twitch due to the pain. The pain—the burning, *ceaseless* pain—controlled his every move. Barbara plucked the shards of glass out of his gashes, one-by-one. The pain slowly subsided.

As she gazed at his abs, Barbara said, "I'll make it feel better, sweetie. Okay? Babs will make it feel better."

"Wha–What are you doing?"

Barbara leaned forward and kissed the gash at the center of Malcolm's abdomen. Malcolm shuddered upon feeling her thin, wrinkly lips.

Before he could say a word, the old woman licked a circle around the gash. She tasted his blood, but it didn't stop her. She lifted her dress and shoved one hand down her underwear. She masturbated in front of him.

Malcolm drew his hips back and cried, "No. Stop it!"

"It's okay. No one will ever know. This... This room isn't part of society, remember? Let me taste you."

With her tongue protruding from her mouth, Barbara lowered her head and licked his torso down to his underwear. She moaned as she rubbed her clitoris.

Malcolm shouted, "Stop it, damn it!"

Barbara cocked her head back. She scowled and pouted, simultaneously angry and disappointed by his rejection. She pulled her hand out of her panties and rubbed her fingers on Malcolm's lips. Malcolm coughed and retched as he felt her moist, stinky fingers. *You sick bitch,* he thought, *you're just as bad as that old bastard.*

Barbara muttered to herself as she cleaned his wounds with some antiseptic wipes. She didn't take the rejection well, but she had a job to do. She stopped caring about his pain, though. After disinfecting his lacerations, she wrapped a gauze bandage around his body. She covered the gash at the center of his abdomen since it was the most severe wound on his torso, excluding his broken bones.

She sneered at him as she moved up to his face. She cleaned his cuts, then she placed a Band-Aid over the gash on his cheek.

With bitterness in her voice, Barbara said, "*There.* You're all patched up, hun. Now you have to eat." The meal was the same as the last one: stale chicken soup and water. She shoved a piece of chicken into his mouth and said, "This isn't over. You still have a lot to learn."

As he gnawed on the chewy chicken, Malcolm asked, "Grandma, can you help me?"

"I just tried to help you and you *rejected* me, didn't you?"

"Not that type of help. I mean, can you... can you do something, *anything,* for me? Please? Like... call my mom or let me out of this thing?"

"No, I'm afraid I can't."

"You can't just leave me like this. I'm hurt."

"I know, I know, but..."

Barbara sighed. She couldn't stay mad at her grandson.

She said, "Here's what I'll do for you, sweetie: I'll leave that towel under your knee. It'll help with the pain. That's the only one you get, though. I'm not a monster, but I'm not a pushover, either."

Barbara shoved two more pieces of chicken and some chopped carrots into his mouth. The food was cold and hard, but he choked it down.

Malcolm asked, "Is there anything else you can do? He, um... He loves you. Can't you convince him to let me stay upstairs?"

Barbara smiled, shrugged, and responded, "The whole point of you being down here is to help you. You're in a good position right now. Don't ruin it."

"He's not helping me. He's only hurting me. Can't

you see that? Look at me, grandma."

"I see everything and I'm proud of you. Pain will turn you into a man and you're handling it well, even if you cry a little too much."

Barbara poured around eight ounces of water into Malcolm's mouth. Some of the water flowed down his chin and streamed down to his chest. For a second, he felt revitalized.

Barbara continued, "I know it might be difficult to believe, but I was once a *stupid* woman. Really, it's true. I was young, wild, and naive. Then, I met your grandfather. He put me through some pain, I hated him for that, but then I became a strong, *smart* woman. I learned a lot from him and I... I just never stopped loving him after that. Cute story, right?"

"If you were really a strong woman, you would have stood up to him. If you're strong, *prove it*. Get me out of here, grandma."

"Ronnie made me into a strong woman. He gave me that gift. So, I would never stab him in the back. I believe in honor, loyalty, and respect. You'll learn all about that, soon."

"Damn it," Malcolm muttered, tears leaking from his bloodshot eyes. He said, "Grandma, you're not acting right. Can't you see that? This... This isn't normal! You're supposed to bake cookies! You're supposed to cook great food during the holidays! You're supposed to love me!"

Barbara frowned and said, "I love you, little Malcolm, but Ronnie is right about you. You need to be disciplined. I know this all seems unfair to you right now, but this is for the greater good. Trust us, baby."

Barbara shoved the last piece of chicken into Malcolm's mouth. Malcolm cried as he chewed on the stale food. *For the greater good,* he thought, *it's bullshit, it's all bullshit.* Barbara poured the rest of the water into his mouth. Her official duties were complete. Deviant ideas still crawled through her mind, though.

Barbara gently tapped his lower abdomen and said, "I know you're angry and ashamed, but... If you need it, I can help you 'relieve' some stress."

Malcolm huffed and shook his head, disgusted by the offer. He fought the urge to spit in her face. The woman healed him, but she was a confused, deviant little thing.

Stony-faced, Malcolm said, "Just get out. Leave me alone."

"Okay, okay. Maybe next time. I'll be back later."

Barbara reluctantly gathered her supplies and exited the bunker. She locked the door and turned off the light.

Malcolm's cold, steady expression broke into a grimace as he sobbed. The pain from his knees, broken ribs, and sliced back blended with his emotional anguish to create the ultimate concoction of agony. He was absolutely devastated.

Six hours, which felt like six days, passed in the bunker.

In that time, Malcolm dozed in-and-out of consciousness, he vomited a thick, creamy liquid, he pissed himself, and he watched as the rats ate his puke and blood. He felt sick, the food didn't do him any favors, but he still tried to save his energy. He stopped screaming, he stopped fighting.

As he stared at the rats, he whispered, "This... is... hell. I'm dead. I'm really... dead."

"Malcolm," a soft feminine voice said.

Malcolm lifted his head and glanced around, his brow raised in curiosity. He couldn't look back because of the pillory, but that didn't matter. The voice came from the corner to his left. He recognized the voice, too, but he couldn't believe it. His bottom lip quivered, his legs trembled, and his shoulders shuddered.

He stuttered, "M–Mom?"

He gasped as a figure moved in the darkness—*a person*. The figure grew larger as it slowly slid forward. He couldn't see the person's body, but he saw part of her face. He could only see her well-defined jaw and mouth. It was enough for him.

Eyes glimmering with hope, he enthusiastically said, "Mom! Mom, you came for me. I missed you so much. Those people, my grandparents, they've been abusing me. They beat me, they cut me, and they even molested me. You have to get me out of this thing before he comes back. Please hurry."

Jennifer did not respond. She stood in silence, enigmatic and motionless. She didn't appear to be breathing, either.

In a strained voice, Malcolm said, "I'm sorry, mom. I'm sorry for everything. I was just so stupid. I know that now. Will you... Will you forgive me? Can you save me?"

Jennifer said, "I'm coming, Malcolm. Give me time."

"It... It really is you," Malcolm said, awed. "How long? When will you get here?"

"Soon."

"When, mom? When?"

Malcolm saw the tear rolling down his mother's cheek. It dripped from her jaw and *plopped* on the ground. It sounded real, but he still questioned his sanity.

Jennifer said, "Soon, Malcolm. Stay strong, baby."

As she slid back to the corner, Malcolm shouted, "Wait! Don't leave me! I'm... I'm scared, mom. Don't leave me here." The figure vanished in the corner of the room. Malcolm lowered his head and whispered, "Mom, I love you..."

Chapter Twenty-Three

The Rope Trick

Malcolm awoke to a bloodcurdling shriek—a long, loud, and raspy scream. The screeching terrified him, causing the hairs at the back of his neck to prickle. He looked to his left, then to his right. He couldn't see anyone in the darkness, though. Fifteen seconds passed until it finally struck him. *He* was the source of the shriek. He was lightheaded and out of breath due to his own screaming. The shriek lowered in volume until it finally stopped.

Wide-eyed, he whispered, "Wha–What happened? What... Why was I screaming?"

He couldn't remember any recent nightmares. As a matter of fact, he couldn't even remember falling asleep. The moments before the shriek were wiped from his memory.

He muttered, "I'm really losing it..."

The bunker was hot, stuffy, and dark. Only the sound of scurrying footsteps emerged in the room— rats searching for food. An acrid stench stained the bunker. The urine, puke, feces, and blood created the vile aroma. The sweat and rats contributed to the stench, too. The bunker had only been occupied for a few days, but it looked like it had been vandalized for months.

Malcolm squinted as a slit of light pierced the darkness from the crack under the door. Then, the light in the bunker turned on and washed the darkness away. As soon as the door swung open, a filthy rat dashed into the room. The teenager didn't understand their purpose. He turned his attention to his visitor.

Ronald entered the room and said, "I told you I'd be back." He dropped a duffel bag on the floor in front of the pillory as he examined the mess. He sneered in disgust and muttered, "You nasty little shit, look at this mess. Goddammit..."

Ashamed, Malcolm whispered, "I'm sorry."

Ronald left the room for a minute, then he returned with a towel. He threw the towel on the floor and he pushed it with his boot to mop the piss and puke. The towel absorbed most of the urine, but it couldn't soak up the thick vomit. He created a bigger mess under the pillory.

He said, "I don't talk about my time in Vietnam often. I'm not embarrassed or ashamed or scared. No, boy, I'm actually proud. It's just... personal." Hands on his knees, he leaned forward and gazed into Malcolm's eyes. He said, "In this bunker, in this particular situation, you remind me of myself. I was put in a cell much smaller than this. I was harassed, I was beaten, I was starved. The only food they gave us was rotten and it was hard to keep down. I threw it up one day and this little Vietcong bastard forced me to eat my own vomit."

Malcolm breathed deeply through his gaping mouth. He glanced down at the puke, then at his grandfather. He thought: *he's not going to make me eat it, is he?*

Ronald continued, "I didn't mind because I'm a man. You understand? Real men do what they have to do in order to survive and thrive. They don't bitch and complain. Hell, at one point, I even ate a friend's vomit out of starvation. I proved myself... and so will you."

He casually threw the soaked towel over Malcolm's head. Malcolm panted as he frantically shook his head, trying to stop the towel from touching his mouth. The urine moistened his face while the clumps of vomit clung to his hair. He even tasted some of the piss on his chapped lips. He retched, but he couldn't vomit.

Ronald pulled the towel off his head. As Malcolm gasped for air and coughed, he shoved a glob of creamy puke into the teenager's mouth. He pushed up on Malcolm's chin with his left hand and grabbed his neck with the other.

He hissed, "Swallow it, boy."

Malcolm grimaced and shook his head as he tasted the sour puke. Tears filled his bloodshot eyes and trickled down his cheeks. Slimy mucus dripped from his nostrils as he snorted and groaned. He struggled to breathe because of his grandfather's grip on his neck.

I don't have a choice, he thought. He stopped shaking his head, he stopped resisting. He tightly squeezed his eyes shut and swallowed the vomit.

Ronald released his grip on his jaw and neck. He chuckled, then he said, "Look at yourself, you dirty little bastard. You swallowed your puke. You gave up and you actually swallowed it. Sick son of a bitch... You're out of energy, aren't you? So soon? You're pathetic. How long do you think you've been here? What day is it, boy? Tell me."

Malcolm drew deep, shaky breaths. He struggled to compose himself. The forced consumption of his puke addled his mind. *Day,* he thought, *what day is it?* He couldn't remember the current month, let alone the day. He thought about telling his grandfather about his hallucination in order to gain some sympathy. *He won't care about that, either,* he thought, *he's going to kill me.*

Ronald pulled a water bottle out of the bag. He dumped the water on Malcolm's face. He didn't scold Malcolm for trying to drink the water, either.

He threw the bottle on the floor and said, "Enough of that. I'm going to release you from this pillory, but you won't be leaving this room. You won't even stand up. I just want to show you a trick I learned in Vietnam."

Ronald nonchalantly unlatched the pillory and lifted the top-half of the horizontal post up. Malcolm lifted his head and arms, amazed. He instantly felt some relief across his neck and wrists. Ronald turned his attention to the bag, unperturbed by his grandson's newfound freedom. He pulled two rolls of rope out of the bag.

While he was busy, Malcolm seized the opportunity and tried to escape. He dipped his head under the pillory and lunged forward, hoping to crawl out of the bunker. He imagined himself escaping the room, then locking his grandfather in the bunker—but that didn't happen. He immediately fell forward and landed face-first on the concrete. He couldn't crawl on his busted knees and his sore wrists couldn't hold him up.

Ronald chuckled, then he muttered, "Stupid boy."

He grabbed Malcolm's ankles and dragged him back, pulling him behind the pillory. He said, "Let's get started."

Sluggish, Malcolm mumbled, "Please, I–I'm... I'm sorry."

Disregarding the apology, Ronald tied Malcolm's legs together at the ankles. He gripped Malcolm's shoulder and pulled him back, lifting him from the ground and forcing him to stand on his knees again. Pain surged from every inch of his body, but Malcolm didn't resist. He breathed deeply as he cried softly.

Ronald pulled Malcolm's arms behind his back and bound his wrists together with a handcuff knot using the second roll of rope. He pulled back on the rope, pulling Malcolm's arms away from his body.

He said, "The Vietcong loved this trick. They'd perform it on their prisoners after breaking a leg or two. They'd laugh and cheer, amused by the simple things in life. I certainly didn't like this 'trick' when it was performed on me, but, I must admit, it was fun to watch."

Ronald placed his left foot on Malcolm's shoulder, firmly planting his boot on his mutilated back. He pulled Malcolm's arms back, then he pulled them upward. Malcolm grimaced in pain as he felt indescribable pressure in his shoulders and elbows. The strange sensation frightened him. He knew his arms weren't supposed to move in that direction.

Ronald tugged the rope upward again, causing a deep but muffled *popping* sound to emerge. The rapid *popping* noise was accompanied by a moist *crunching* sound. Malcolm screamed as his shoulders and elbows were popped out of their sockets. Realizing the pain was severe, he finally attempted to fight back. He jerked every which way and tried to lower his arms, but to no avail. He couldn't overpower his grandfather. His struggle only worsened the pain.

Ronald gritted his teeth as he rotated Malcolm's arms upward until his hands were over his head behind him. He pushed down on his back with his foot, too, maximizing the pain. Malcolm felt his muscles tearing and ligaments puncturing. He could even hear faint cracking, popping, and shredding sounds in his shoulders. He felt a burning sensation across his arms, as if acid were flowing through his veins.

Ronald asked, "It hurts, doesn't it?" You want to cry, don't you?"

Malcolm stuttered, "S–S–Stop. It–It hurts..." Ronald tugged on the rope again, pulling his arms higher. His voice raspy, Malcolm shouted, "Stop!"

Malcolm's arms became numb, but he still felt pain in his joints. Beads of sweat rained down from his face and hair, plopping on the ground. His face, neck, and shoulders turned blood-red. After three minutes, Ronald released his grip on the rope. Malcolm's limp arms fell down, still tied behind his back. Blood flowed back into his limp limbs, increasing the pain tenfold. Malcolm sobbed as he fell forward.

Before he could hit the floor, Ronald grabbed his shoulder and stopped him. He untied the rope around his wrists and ankles while holding him up.

The old man chuckled, then he said, "You would

have knocked yourself out if you hit the floor like that. You need to stay conscious, though. You've made it too far to quit. You're almost a man. Now, let me give you a hand."

Malcolm breathed shakily, rendered lethargic by the brutal abuse. Hundreds of thoughts ran through his mind, stampeding over each other in his head: *where am I? Why am I here? What did I do to deserve this?*

Ronald crouched behind Malcolm. He grabbed the teenager's right arm at the bicep and his wrist, then he popped his elbow back into place. Malcolm gasped and trembled. Saliva dripped from his mouth, tears streamed down his rosy cheeks. He didn't have time to recover, though. His grandfather quickly popped his shoulder back into place.

Ronald popped his left elbow into place, but he couldn't do the same for his shoulder. He couldn't get a good grip on his grandson's moist arm.

He stood up and said, "Your grandmother will fix this one up later. If not... Well, one arm is better than none. It'll teach you something about gratitude." He placed Malcolm into the pillory again, locking him into place. As he gathered his supplies, he said, "You still have a few more tests. You've shown heart and strength, but this isn't over. I'll be back to show you another Vietcong favorite."

Malcolm watched with hopeless eyes as his grandfather exited the bunker. The light went out, the rats scurried about, and the cold sensation of utter desolation returned. It was the new 'normal' for Malcolm, and he hated it.

Chapter Twenty-Four

The Tiger Cage

Malcolm opened his eyes slowly, surprised and relieved. For the first time in what felt like days, he awoke without screaming or pissing himself. His eyes as narrow as coin slots, he stared at the doorway in front of him. The door was open and light entered the room from the main basement. The light in the bunker was off, though.

He spotted two figures standing near the doorway. One of them was short and round, the other was bulky and a bit taller—*his grandparents.* Although their voices were muffled, he heard bits and pieces of their conversation.

Barbara said, "Ronnie, honey, I don't know about this. He's hurt badly. He might... He might die down here."

"Don't say that," Ronald responded, his voice filled with confidence. "I know what I'm doing, Babs. I've been through this before, you've been through this. He's not going to die under my watch. I can guarantee that."

"But look at him. He looks so bad, doesn't he? What if he does die? What will happen to us? Are we going to–"

"Shut your mouth, woman. I told you: he is *not* going to die. If he is Jenny's son, if he has my blood flowing through him, he'll survive. I'm from a bloodline of survivors—of fighters. Now, if his blood-father tainted him with his wetback genes, then it would be better if he died anyway. Right? *Right?*"

Malcolm could see his grandmother trembling with fear—or was it excitement? He couldn't read Barbara like a normal person because she was abnormal.

Barbara said, "You're right. I'm sorry."

Ronald responded, "Don't ever question me again."

"Okay, Ronnie."

"Now, turn on the bunker light, get the food, and follow the plan."

"Okay."

Ronald entered the bunker. He crossed his arms and leaned back on the wall next to the door. Barbara flicked a switch, she grabbed the tray of food, and she entered the bright bunker. Malcolm watched her as she knelt down in front of him. *Don't touch me,* he thought, *please don't touch me in front of him.*

Barbara asked, "How are you doing, baby?"

In a hoarse voice, Malcolm responded, "I need to go... to a hospital. I can't feel my left arm, grandma. My legs... My legs are killing me, too." He looked over at his grandfather, eyes like a puppy's. He said, "Please take me to a hospital."

Ronald didn't answer him. He stared at the boy and waited for his wife to complete her duties.

Barbara said, "You don't need a hospital, silly boy. You're an O'Donnell, so you'll heal quickly. Doctors... They don't know as much as you think." She smiled and said, "Look, I brought you something fresh to eat."

A plate with chicken breasts and white rice, a slice of toast with butter, and a cup of water sat on the tray. Barbara fed Malcolm the food. To his utter surprise, it was actually fresh and delicious. His tongue quivered with excitement as his taste buds tingled. He savored the first fresh meal of the week. The water relieved the pain in his throat, too.

After the meal, Barbara wiped Malcolm's privates and ass with a wet towel. She didn't dare fondle him in front of Ronald, though. It wasn't a good time for molestation.

Ronald said, "Alright, that'll keep him alive. You've done enough, Babs."

Barbara grabbed her tray and stepped away from the pillory. She said, "Okay, he's ready for you."

Ronald approached Malcolm and said, "Solitary confinement, the hole, purgatory... Whatever you want to call it, this is the ultimate form of psychological discipline. Your mind deteriorates when it's isolated. It crumbles until there's nothing left. I can see your mind hasn't completely deteriorated, boy, so I can't start rebuilding you... *yet.*" He tapped the pillory and said, "Things can always get worse. You think it's bad now, but you've had a lot of benefits in this position. You could wiggle around, move your head and thrust your hips, and you could even shift your weight from one knee to the other."

He smirked as he stared down at Malcolm's knees. His right knee was wrapped in a bloody bandage, sitting on top of a folded towel. His other knee was black and blue, bruised by the rough floor.

Ronald said, "In this position, your knees are the only part of your body that really suffered. I know how to make it worse, though. I can completely isolate you."

Malcolm gazed into his grandfather's excited eyes. He thought: *my back, my ribs, my entire body has suffered, you bastard.* He was reinvigorated by the food, but he decided to save his energy. Escape was his primary objective. Vengeance could wait.

Ronald continued, "In Vietnam, prisoners were placed in 'tiger cages.' These were tiny cells without roofs. The guards would watch their tortured prisoners from above while depriving them of food and water. We're going to combine total isolation and tiger cages for a new form of discipline."

Malcolm clenched his jaw and nodded. He was afraid, but he still had to wait for the perfect opportunity to retaliate. Ronald smiled, pleasantly surprised. He believed his experiment was working.

Ronald unlatched the pillory and lifted the top-half of the horizontal post. He hooked his arms under Malcolm's armpits and dragged him back to the other side of the room. Then, he carefully laid the boy down between the holes that were drilled into the ground. Malcolm remembered seeing the holes during his first visit to the bunker. As he examined the holes, he thought: *they were for a cage, he's done this before, this was always part of his plan.*

Ronald beckoned to Barbara and said, "Get on him. I'll be back with the cage in a minute."

Malcolm gasped as Barbara straddled his hips. He could feel the warmth from her crotch on his groin.

She was wearing a white nightgown, and he only hoped she was also wearing underwear. Ronald exited the bunker and headed upstairs. His armory of torture tools was located in the attic.

Malcolm turned his attention to his grandmother. He sneered upon noticing the smirk on her face. He gently thrust his hips up, trying to measure Barbara's weight. To his dismay, she was too heavy to lift with a thrust. He couldn't knock her off of him without a loud and painful struggle.

Barbara snickered, then she said, "Malcolm, honey, you can't do that now. Listen, when this is over, we'll have all the fun you want. Okay?"

Malcolm realized his grandmother had misconstrued his thrust. He thought about escape and vengeance while Barbara thought about sex with her grandson. It was a disgusting idea.

Clanking and *thudding* sounds emerged in the basement. The pair looked over at the doorway. Ronald returned with a rusty, human-sized cage. Malcolm recognized the cage from the attic. He instantly regretted his failure to act. *I should have destroyed all of his shit when I had the chance,* he thought.

Ronald said, "Get up."

Barbara covered her mouth and blushed as she stood up. Ronald placed the cage over Malcolm, then he examined it from top to bottom.

He said, "It's the perfect fit. If you were an inch taller, I would have had to cut off your feet." He chuckled, then he said, "Now don't move. If you make me fuck this up, I'll drill *you* to the floor."

Ronald pulled a power-drill out of a bag. One-by-one, he slid nails through the frame of the cage, then he drilled the nails into the concrete. The cage was nailed to the floor *over* Malcolm's body.

Malcolm tightly closed his eyes and grimaced as the sound of the drill irritated his sensitive ears. He couldn't raise his arms up to his head to cover his ears, despite his efforts. He couldn't turn over to rest on his side or stomach, either. The cage was less than two feet tall and two-and-a-half feet wide, so his ability to move was restricted. He lay on concrete, so his bare back ached—from his sliced shoulders to his mutilated ass. The position was worse than the pillory.

After drilling the final nail, Ronald stood up and swiped the sweat from his brow. He walked around the cage, staring down at his grandson with sharp eyes. He examined every detail, searching for any weaknesses. The cage was old and rusty, but it was secured by the nails. He couldn't help but smile. Malcolm reminded him of his time in Vietnam—the good ol' days.

Ronald said, "You'll be staying in this cage for a while, boy. If we decide to feed you, you'll be fed through a straw. If you piss or shit yourself in there, you'll have to sleep in your filth. We're not cleaning it up. In other words, you better be ready for a few days of true isolation. If you survive... Well, we'll talk about that *if* it happens." He pointed at the foot of the cage. He said, "And, by the way, I left a small gap down there for your little 'friends.' When they start starving, they'll eat each other or... or they'll eat something else."

"Fr–Friends?" Malcolm stuttered.

Ronald grinned and said, "Good luck, boy."

"Bye-bye, hun," Barbara said as she waved.

Malcolm watched as his grandparents exited the bunker. The door was locked, then the light vanished. He groaned as he squirmed on the ground and glanced every which way. He couldn't find a comfortable position. His grandfather's words echoed through his mind: *for your little friends, little friends, little friends.* He didn't understand him.

He closed his eyes and tried to sleep by counting sheep. At the very least, he felt some comfort in knowing he wouldn't suffocate in his sleep. *One sheep, two sheep, three sheep...*

Chapter Twenty-Five

Agony

Malcolm stared vacantly at the darkness above the tiger cage. Time was nonexistent in the bunker, but he knew it had been hours since he was placed in the cage. *Twelve hours,* he thought, *no, it's been much longer than that.* He moaned and wiggled on the ground. He felt like he fell down a flight of stairs, aching from head-to-toe due to the concrete floor.

He whispered, "I have to get out of here. I can't just lay here and die."

He took a deep breath and grabbed the cage with his right hand—his only good hand—then he pushed upward. The cage rattled, but it did not budge. He loosened his grip and caught his breath. He tightened his grip and pressed his left knee against the cage, then he pushed upward once more, exhausting all of his energy.

Yet again, the cage rattled and the frame screeched, but it did not budge. The cage was securely fastened to the ground.

"Shit," Malcolm muttered as he stopped pushing.

He sighed in disappointment. He felt strong thanks to the fresh food, but he was afraid of wasting that energy. At the same time, if he didn't escape soon, he feared his newfound energy would go to waste. He was caught in a complicated predicament, forced to play a game of survival against a ruthless man. There were no rules, either.

It was a free-for-all—and he was losing.

Malcolm whispered, "What do I do? I mean, shit, what would a 'real' man do? What would my... my real dad do?"

He tried to roll over to reduce the pain on his back. His left arm and shoulder scraped the top of the cage and stopped him.

Frustrated, he shouted, "Damn it! I can't do this anymore! I can't even sleep!" He tried to raise his hand up to his face to rub his eyes, but he couldn't even reach his head because of the short height of the cage. He said, "You have to be kidding me... Why is this happening to me? Why?"

Warm, salty tears rolled from his eyes to his ears. He snorted and coughed as mucus filled his nostrils. Short, panicked breaths flowed out of his mouth.

His eyes closed and his voice cracking, he said, "I'm sorry for all of the stupid shit I've done. I know it doesn't matter now, but I... I never meant to hurt anyone. I–I just did it because I wanted attention. I wanted to–to be cool, too. I wanted people to like me, but I was afraid of doing it any other way. I was just so stupid." He sniffled and groaned, releasing his emotional pain through his tears. He said, "I love you, mom. I love you so much. I never stopped thinking about you and I–I never blamed you for this. You're the best mom ever. I–I love my friends, too. Marcus, Alex, Gaby, Maribel, David... everyone who cared about me at school. And... And, I *really* liked Claire. I know I didn't know her that much, but I... I cared about her. I felt like I could have... *loved* her. I never got to tell her how I feel. I'll never be able to tell anyone about any of this! None of it!"

He shook his head and sobbed. He mumbled indistinctly, apologizing for all of his foolish actions. Bittersweet memories of the past flashed in his mind, regret burdened his shoulders, and guilt festered in his heart. Fear flowed through his veins and rippled through his body as the most terrifying thought crept into his mind: *death is certain.*

He stuttered, "I–I don't want to–to die. I–I'm scared. What's going to happen? What... What happens when I die? Do I go to heaven? Or hell? Does it all just go... black? Is it nothing? Is it better than this?" He threw a tantrum, flopping on the ground while hitting the cage with his arms and legs. He shouted, "No! It's not fair! I don't want to die, damn it! Please, don't let me–"

Ow!—he yelped upon feeling a sharp pain in his foot. The pain started in his big toe, it surged across his leg like an electric jolt, then the pain slowly dwindled. He still felt something scratching at his toe, though. Then, the sharp pain emerged again, emanating from the gummy skin under his toenail. He felt a warm liquid dribbling down the bottom of his foot. *Blood*—it was the first thought that entered his mind.

"Oh, shit. Why am I bleeding?" he muttered.

He jerked his waist to the right and moved his head to the left. He stared down at his foot, baffled. He couldn't see through the darkness, but he heard a faint munching sound. His breathing intensified as horrific ideas ran through his mind. He thought: *my sores are leaking, I'm going to lose a leg if I survive, I'm actually rotting while I'm still alive.* Finally, he spotted the culprit behind his foot—a filthy rat.

He screamed and kicked his foot up, knocking the rat back. The rat swiftly rolled back to its feet, then it dashed towards Malcolm's left foot. It gripped its foot with its tiny hands and munched on his big toe. Malcolm tried to kick the rat off of him again, but the rat's teeth were attached firmly to his toe. It clawed at the bottom and sides of his foot, too, refusing to loosen its grip.

Malcolm shouted, "Help! Grandma! Grand–"

The sound of the rattling cage interrupted him—*clink, clink, clink.* He looked down at his feet and gasped. Another rat entered the tiger cage from the hole at the bottom. Ronald's words finally made sense to him. *They're starved, so they were either going to eat each other or me,* he thought, *and they picked me.*

The second rat chomped on his right index finger, easily puncturing his skin. The third and fourth rats entered the cage. One of them joined the rat on his left foot, clawing and chewing at his sole. The other rat hopped onto his broken knee. It scratched at the old bandage around his busted knee like a dog digging a hole, then it stuffed its face inside and chewed *into* the gash on his kneecap.

Malcolm screamed and swung his right arm. The rat on his finger crashed into the ceiling of the cage, then it landed on his stomach. He felt its feet and hands pricking his abdomen as it dashed towards his face. Before it reached his neck, he swiped it off his chest. The rat retreated, opting to attack Malcolm's left hand instead.

As he flailed his limbs, Malcolm shouted, "Help me! Somebody help me! Please! *Please!*"

He hissed and groaned as he felt sharp pain across his legs and arms. Blood leaked from his wounds as the rats chewed through his flesh. The process would be slow and painful, it was difficult to imagine, but he was actually being eaten alive by starved rats. He could hear the moist *crunching* and *popping* sounds as they broke through his toenails and clawed at his soles.

He couldn't stop his right leg from shaking. The rat's entire head was *inside* of his knee, feasting on his blood, ligaments, and tendons.

His voice raspy, he croaked, "H–Help... Help me..."

A rat reached his left ear. The rat clawed at his cheek, then it turned its attention to his ear. It chewed on his earlobe.

Malcolm couldn't reach the rat with his hand due to the small, tight cage. He dropped his arms to his side and accepted defeat. He figured the rat near his ear would eventually eat his eyes, then his face, and then his neck. The others would eat him from his toes to his chest. He would likely bleed out before they could get that far, though. He had the energy to fight, but he believed the situation was hopeless. He couldn't muster the courage to continue fighting. It was over.

As he stared up at the ceiling, rats gnawing on his flesh, Malcolm whispered, "Just kill me already..."

Chapter Twenty-Six

Retribution

A *click* and a *clack* emerged in the bunker, then the door cracked open. A wide beam of white light entered the room. It wasn't the basement or bunker light, though.

Malcolm lay in the cage with his eyes closed, rats chewing on his body and enjoying a feast of human flesh. Although he heard the noise and saw the light through his eyelids, he refused to open his eyes. He believed his grandparents had entered the room to watch him cry and die. He didn't want to give them any satisfaction. The sound of a *thudding* footstep followed, then he heard a loud gasp.

Malcolm thought: *they wouldn't gasp at this.* He realized someone else was in the bunker with him.

"Malcolm," a soft, feminine voice said. "Oh my God, what did they do to you?"

Malcolm opened his eyes and glanced over at the door. The bright light from a flashlight blinded him. The light grew stronger as the intruder ran towards the cage.

Upon recognizing the voice, Malcolm weakly whispered, "Wa–Wait a second. I... I know you. It–It's not possible."

Peering through the light, he finally recognized the intruder's face. A grin stretched across his swollen face as tears of joy gushed from his eyes.

Claire Olson knelt down beside the cage,

examining Malcolm's wounds in utter horror. She illuminated his bumps, bruises, bite marks, cuts, and open sores. His skin looked sickly pale and his lips were discolored, too.

Her voice cracking with fear, Claire cried, "Oh, God, wha–what happened? How... How did this happen?"

Still grinning, Malcolm asked, "Are you real?"

Claire responded, "Yes. Yes, Malcolm, I'm real. Oh, shit, look at yourself. There are..." She held her hands over her mouth and shuddered as she looked at the rats. She said, "They're eating you. Holy shit, they're actually eating you. This... This is unbelievable. This is insane."

She struck the bottom of the cage with the handle of the flashlight. The rats fell off of Malcolm's mangled foot. She hit the cage again, scaring off the starved rats.

Malcolm said, "I thought he shot you. I thought you were dead."

Claire grabbed the cage near Malcolm's face and leaned forward. Half a smile on her face—a smile of pain and relief—she said, "I thought you were dead, too, Malcolm."

"Yeah? Well, he almost got me. I... I actually gave up just before you got here. I was, um... I was really ready to die."

"No. Don't give up. Don't *ever* give up. I'm here now, okay? I'm going to get you out of here."

Malcolm's bottom lip quivered as he fought the urge to cry. Claire's words of reassurance rekindled his hope. Her mere presence proved that he was worthy of life and love. She risked everything to enter the O'Donnell house in order to find him. They truly cared about each other.

Claire tugged on the cage and asked, "How do I get this thing off of you?"

"It's... drilled to the floor. You have to... to cut through it. Go back to the other room and grab some... some pliers from the workbench. That should do it."

"Okay. I'll be right back."

Claire struck the cage again with the flashlight, causing the rats to scurry to a corner. She tiptoed out of the bunker and approached the workbench in the basement. She ran the light over the hammers, screwdrivers, wrenches, and drills. She grabbed a pair of pliers and ran back to the bunker. On her knees, she cut through the cage near the frame, wire-by-wire.

Malcolm whispered, "Try to keep it down. They might hear you."

Claire cut through another wire and explained, "I'll try, but they should be asleep right now anyway."

"What time is it?"

"It was, uh... eleven when I came in here."

"Eleven?"

"Yeah," Claire responded through her gritted teeth as she tightly squeezed the handles of the pliers and twisted her wrists. She moved on to another wire and said, "I snuck in here through the back door. It took me forever to pick that lock."

Malcolm chuckled, then he asked, "You learned how to pick locks?"

Claire cracked a smile and said, "Yeah. It took a

214

few days to get a hang of it, but I did it. All of the lights were off when I came in. I thought I heard someone moving around upstairs, but... I don't know. I think they're sleeping."

Malcolm tried to keep the smile on his face. He didn't want to frighten his girlfriend with a stony-faced expression. However, the circumstances seemed suspicious. He remembered his first night at the house—he stumbled upon his grandparents having rough sex. It was possible that they were upstairs at the moment, completely conscious and completely naked.

Claire continued, "I called the cops before I broke in. I called them a few days ago, too, but they ignored me. They said they were already looking for you because you ran away."

"My grandpa... He told them that."

"Well, this time, I called and I used my mom's name. I told them that I heard yelling and crying over here."

"Good, that's good. How... How long has it been? How long have I been here, Claire?"

"I don't know. It's been a week at least."

"A week? Are you sure?"

"Maybe a little longer."

Malcolm turned his attention to the ceiling, flabbergasted. He felt like he spent seven years in the bunker. He was killed, reborn, killed again, then resurrected. *One week,* he thought, *that can't be right, can it?*

Claire cut through the last wire. She carefully lifted the cage from the frame, trying to limit the noise, then she placed it against the wall. *Shoo, shoo*

—she kicked at the rats, but she didn't actually hit them. She stood over Malcolm and frowned as she examined his wounds. His feet were mauled by the rats, but he could walk on them. She was concerned about his bandaged leg, though.

She shone the light at his mutilated kneecap and asked, "How bad is it? Can you walk?"

"It's bad. It's very bad," Malcolm responded. He grimaced as he sat up. He reached for Claire and said, "I can limp, though. Help me up."

Claire took a deep breath and nodded. She dashed to Malcolm's side. She threw his arm over her shoulder, she grabbed his waist with a firm grip, then she helped him stand.

Malcolm hissed and panted in pain. His right leg, bloody and broken, hurt with the slightest movement. A stinging pain emerged in his ankles, too. It was his first time standing on his feet in over a week. The pain was expected.

Claire said, "Come on. Let's get you out of here. The police should be here soon and... and I'll call an ambulance outside. We just have to get you far away from this place first. It's over, Malcolm. It's finally over."

Malcolm couldn't help but cry as he limped out of the bunker. He felt overjoyed, revitalized, and liberated. *I'm out of purgatory, but she's wrong,* he thought, *it's not over.* He stopped moving before they could reach the stairs.

Claire asked, "What's wrong? We have to go, Malcolm."

"We need weapons. If they're awake, if *he's* awake, there's no way we're getting past them like

216

this. Grab something from the workbench."

"Are you serious? They're old. I can hit him with the flashlight and he–"

"*No.* You might be able to beat my grandma, but that old man is strong. Look at me, Claire. Look at me... He did this to me. We're going to need weapons."

Claire bit her bottom lip and nodded, as if to say: *I'm not sure about this, but okay.* She led Malcolm to the workbench. They took a moment to examine the tools—to analyze the situation. They were picking weapons to attack their elders after all. Malcolm chose a claw hammer while Claire grabbed a monkey wrench.

Claire shoved the wrench into her waistband and whispered, "Okay, let's go."

The couple headed up the stairs. Claire leaned on the wall while trying to lift Malcolm from the steps below him. Malcolm grimaced as he hopped up the stairs on one foot, his damaged shoulder gliding across the wall. He felt pain across every inch of his body. He nearly slipped because of the blood leaking from his soles.

One minute, two minutes, *three minutes*—it took them three minutes to reach the top. Claire squeezed her way to Malcolm's side. They looked at each other, they shared a smile, then they nodded— *let's do it.*

***

Claire opened the door while keeping one hand on Malcolm's waist. They stood in the doorway, pleasantly surprised. The front door stood directly across from them, closed and locked. Darkness filled the house, allowing a dark, malevolent aura to linger in the home. Slits of moonlight barely penetrated the blinds and curtains over the windows. The light couldn't conjure any comfort.

Claire and Malcolm took one step forward, then they stopped. They heard a whistle and a clank. They looked over at the kitchen archway, eyes wide with fear. *The kettle,* Malcolm thought.

As they took another step forward, Barbara emerged in the kitchen archway, a teacup and saucer in her hands. Her blue bathrobe was open in front, and she was nude underneath it. Her sagging breasts, round stomach, and bushy pubic hair were flaunted like a rapper's wealth. She held the teacup close to her thin lips, but she didn't take a sip.

Barbara stared at Malcolm and Claire and Malcolm and Claire stared back at Barbara. Their mouths were open, but they didn't utter a sound.

Tears coursing down his cheeks, Malcolm shook Claire's shoulder and said, "Get her. Knock her out. Do something, Claire."

Claire pulled the wrench out, but she hesitated. She was caught off guard by Barbara's casual nudity. She couldn't imagine herself striking the frail elderly woman, either.

Barbara yelled, "Ronnie! Ronnie, he's out! Oh, Christ Almighty, he's out!"

Malcolm rushed towards his grandmother, his damaged legs wobbling under him. In a knee-jerk reaction, Barbara threw the tea at Malcolm. The hot liquid splashed on his arms and chest. His skin immediately reddened and peeled. The tea didn't stop him, though. He slapped the saucer out of her hands, then he struck her face with a backhanded slap.

Claire gasped upon witnessing the attack. She felt the anger within Malcolm and she spotted the sly malevolence in the elderly woman. She watched as Malcolm slapped her again, then they stumbled into the kitchen. She furrowed her brow and looked up at the ceiling. She heard loud, heavy footsteps coming from the second floor.

Ronald was on the move. His footsteps emerged from the master bedroom, then they appeared to move up a flight of stairs. Claire thought: *he's going to the attic, but why?* She ran to the kitchen to warn Malcolm. She saw him strangling and slapping his grandmother near the stove. Meanwhile, Barbara dug her fingernails into the cuts on Malcolm's abdomen. Blood streamed down her fingers and covered her hands as the gashes widened.

Claire shouted, "Malcolm, we have to go! She's not worth it!"

Malcolm gazed into his grandmother's zany eyes. He wanted to kill her, he wanted vengeance, but he also wanted to live. If Ronald joined the fight, the teens would surely lose. He slapped her again, then he released his grip on her throat. He limped away from her, but the pain from his legs stopped him before he could exit the kitchen. He leaned over a counter, wheezing and groaning.

Claire looked up at the ceiling—Ronald was still preoccupied—then she looked back into the kitchen. Her eyes widened as she spotted Barbara grabbing a knife from a knife block on the counter.

She shouted, "Look out!"

Malcolm turned and gasped as Barbara lifted the knife over her shoulder. He rushed towards his grandmother again. He pushed her back over the counter and grabbed her wrists. The old woman's bathrobe flapped open, revealing her entire torso. She kicked Malcolm's broken shin. The kick was weak on account of her bare foot, but he still felt a powerful twinge.

Claire ran into the kitchen, holding the wrench overhead. She stopped beside the wrestling pair. She swung the wrench down at Barbara's head, but she stopped mid-swing. She saw the sheer fear in the woman's devious eyes. She couldn't read her. *Is she evil? Did she hurt him?*–she thought. She couldn't push herself to physically harm her, but she had to do something.

Her eyes darted to the left, then to the right, then to the left again. Her eyes glowed with hope as an idea materialized in her mind. If she couldn't hurt her, she figured she could scare her away. And fire scared most animals.

Claire turned the knob on the stove and grabbed the belt of Barbara's robe. She held the belt over the hissing flames. The belt was set aflame, and the fire rapidly climbed up the belt until it reached the rest of her robe.

Claire wrapped her arms around Malcolm's waist and shouted, "We have to go!"

"Not yet!" Malcolm barked.

"He's coming!"

"She deserves this!"

Malcolm kicked Barbara's kneecap with the heel of his foot. Barbara's leg snapped with a bone-crunching *pop* and the bloody bone protruded from the back of her knee. Blood gushed out of the open fracture wound. Barbara hopped on her only good foot and howled in pain.

Claire flinched and closed her eyes, shocked by the violence. She pulled Malcolm away from his grandmother. They fell to the ground at the other side of the kitchen. Claire landed on her ass and Malcolm landed on Claire.

Barbara shrieked as she hopped across the room in the burning robe. *Stop, drop, and roll*—the simple concept didn't cross her mind. She didn't even consider removing the robe. The human mind worked in mysterious ways, especially during times of pain and distress. So, she hopped out of the kitchen and spread the fire across the home.

In the living room, she spun wildly as she flailed her arms every which way. Burning pieces of her robe were scattered across the room, landing on the recliner, coffee table, console table, and television. The curtains were set ablaze by the smallest spark. The rug under her feet was even set aflame. She finally collapsed and she tried to roll on the ground, but it was too late—she was swallowed by the fire.

Malcolm and Claire watched in awe from the archway. Claire was burdened by guilt and regret. She wanted to scare the woman, she didn't want to kill her. Malcolm thought: *it was the right thing to do, wasn't it?*

Ronald stood at the bottom of the stairs, eyes wide with anger. He only wore a white tank top and striped boxers. He held a revolver in his right hand. He loaded the gun in the attic, unaware of his wife's suffering. He could see Barbara's twitching body through the powerful flames, but he knew she wasn't moving voluntarily. She was dead, burned to a crisp. Blood leaked from her charred, cracked skin, sizzling due to the immense heat.

Ronald stuttered, "Ba–Babs..."

Malcolm and Claire, arm-in-arm, shambled across the living room, easing their way to the front door.

Ronald screamed and shot at them. The bullet whizzed past them and struck the wall in the dining room. Claire fell forward and Malcolm fell back. Malcolm lurched towards his grandfather. He pushed Ronald's hand up, forcing him to shoot at the ceiling. Malcolm grabbed Ronald's wrists, he pushed his arms over his head, and then he pushed him back. They crashed into the wall beside the basement door.

Ronald shouted, "You're dead, boy! You're dead!"

Pinning his grandfather's arms to the wall, Malcolm glanced back at Claire and shouted, "Get the gun! Hit him! Hurry!"

Claire bolted into action. She screamed as she ran forward. She struck Ronald's right hand with the wrench. The sound of his bones *popping* exploded over the crackling fire. She struck him again, causing the revolver to *clink* in his hand. He howled and hissed, but he did not release his grip on the gun. It was practically glued to his fingers.

Ronald thrust his head forward and tried to headbutt Malcolm. Malcolm dodged the attack, then he thrust his head at Ronald's neck. He hit his throat with a powerful headbutt, causing the old man to gag and cough. He kept his forehead planted on his neck in order to stop him from headbutting him again.

Ronald changed his strategy. He knew Malcolm's weak points. He kicked his battered kneecaps with his bare feet. Malcolm bawled as his legs shook violently. He nearly lost his grip on Ronald's arms. His clammy hands slid down to his forearms.

Malcolm croaked, "Ki-Kill him, Claire... Cave his head in..."

Cave his head in—it sounded so primeval to her, excessively violent and primitive. Instead, she struck Ronald's wrist with the wrench. She grunted and groaned, sweat trickling from her brow because of the heat and exhaustion. One, two, three, four, five... *fifteen*—she hit his wrist fifteen times. A gash formed on his wrist while his skin turned red, blue, and purple.

Finally, the revolver fell from his hand. It hit the floor with a *thump*, which was nearly masked by the roaring fire behind the group.

Claire grabbed the gun and staggered back. She aimed the revolver at the men, but she couldn't pull the trigger. She held the gun with both hands, but she couldn't stop herself from shaking.

Malcolm shouted, "Shoot him!"

Ronald hissed, "Don't do it, girl!"

"Do it!"

"You're dead if you do, cunt! You hear me?!"

As he leaped away from his grandfather, Malcolm shouted, "*Now!*"

Claire closed her eyes and squeezed the trigger. Three booming gunshots echoed through the house. She opened her eyes and gasped. A bullet struck

Ronald's right collarbone. Blood jetted out of the wound like oil from an oil rig blowout. The second bullet hit his abdomen, directly above his bellybutton. Blood leaked out of the wound and streamed down to his boxers. The final round struck the wall beside him.

Ronald took two steps forward, then he collapsed near the basement door. Claire dropped the gun. The shocked expression on her face read: *what have I done?*

Malcolm limped towards her and said, "You did what you had to do. You saved me. Now, let's get the hell out of here."

Claire glanced over at Malcolm, teary-eyed. She nodded and stuttered, "O–Okay, okay."

The couple limped across the living room, coughing as smoke filled their lungs. They exited the house through the front door and tumbled on the front lawn. A cool breeze caressed their warm, sweaty bodies and fresh air filled their lungs.

Malcolm looked back at the house, astonished. The fire could be seen through the first-floor windows, flickering and dancing. Plumes of smoke escaped through the front door, billowing skyward. The sight was hauntingly beautiful. *I'm free,* he thought, *we beat them.*

Claire rubbed Malcolm's shoulder as she glanced around the neighborhood. She spotted an audience of teenagers across the street, recording the scene with their cell phones while gossiping. In their robes, adults stood on their lawns and porches as they watched the O'Donnell house and called the cops.

"Malcolm," Clare said. "Look, the police are here."

A black-and-white police cruiser rolled to a stop in front of the house. A young, blonde-haired police officer—Derrick Duncan—climbed out of the vehicle. His hand on his holster, he approached the front gate with caution.

As Claire tried to help Malcolm to his feet, Duncan said, "Wait. Don't move."

The cop needed a second to assess the situation. A burning house and a pair of injured teenagers could indicate an accident or a case of arson. Judging from the severe wounds on Malcolm's body, he assumed the teenagers were the victims.

As he opened the gate, Duncan asked, "Is there anyone else in the house?"

Malcolm and Claire looked at each other, communicating with their eyes. Claire's eyes said something along the lines of: *it's up to you.* Malcolm looked back at the house, conflicted. *They deserve to die,* he thought, *they deserve to burn in hell.*

Malcolm said, "There's no one in the house. My grandparents are out. They're... They're out."

Duncan approached them and asked, "Are both of you hurt?"

Claire coughed, then she said, "No. I think I'm okay. I just... I think I inhaled some smoke."

"The paramedics will take a look at you," Duncan responded. He clenched his jaw as he examined Malcolm's injuries—bruises, cuts, sores, broken bones. He said, "You're definitely going to need a wagon."

Malcolm continued to stare at the house, pondering the morality of his decision. Claire wiped the tears from her eyes, struggling to bury her guilty conscience. Duncan stood over the couple and reported the situation to his dispatcher. Meanwhile, the neighbors watched the show from afar—one person's tragedy was another's entertainment.

Malcolm raised his brow upon spotting a figure through the doorway. The shadow limped forward, pushing through the grayish-brown clouds of smoke.

Malcolm crawled in reverse and shouted, "He's still alive! Shoot him!"

"Oh, God!" Claire yelled as she looked over at the front door.

Ronald walked onto the porch, blood dripping from his wounds. His eyes were bloodshot and teary, like the eyes of a regretful drunk. His skin was blackened and sooty. A river of blood flowed through his abdominal gunshot wound down to his right kneecap. He held the revolver in his right hand, the barrel aiming at the ground.

Duncan drew his handgun and aimed it at Ronald. He shouted, "Drop the gun! Drop it now!" Ronald took a step forward. Duncan yelled, "Don't move! Drop the gun! Now!"

Blood foaming from his mouth, Ronald said, "I– I'm sorry, officer. I.. I have to finish the... the lesson. I have to make him into a man. His daddy, he ain't going to do it. He's gone."

"Put it down!"

"I have to finish the lesson."

His eyes locked on Malcolm, Ronald placed his finger on the trigger and raised the revolver. Duncan squeezed the trigger, firing three rounds at the porch. One round struck Ronald's right arm at the bicep, the second penetrated his rib cage, and the other flew into the house through the doorway.

Ronald bent over and dropped the revolver. He held his left hand over his ribs while blood squirted from his bicep. He took another step forward, then he collapsed.

Duncan muttered, "Shit..."

He updated his dispatcher as he approached the downed man. He checked Ronald's pulse, then he yelled at the neighbors.

Malcolm didn't hear his words, though. He stared at his grandfather's body. He thought: *is he dead? Is it really over?* His vision began to fade, darkening with each passing second. He looked over at Claire. He saw her flapping lips, but he couldn't hear her. He fell unconscious in her arms, surrounded by chaos.

Chapter Twenty-Seven

The End

Jennifer stood in the doorway of the hospital room, her eyes overflowing with tears. Her son lay on a bed to the left. His broken leg was elevated on an elevation pillow. The wounds on his torso, hands, ear, and ass were properly sutured and bandaged. An IV tube also protruded from his arm. His appearance improved in the hospital, he looked clean and healthy, but she still felt his pain.

Malcolm's eyes lit up as soon as he spotted his mother. He tried to keep a steady expression on his face, but to no avail. His lips quivered, his nose scrunched up, and his eyes watered.

Jennifer ran up to the bed and hugged Malcolm. They cried in each other's arms, releasing their pain through their tears. A reassuring warmth swept through them. It was as if they had met for the first time in years—no, *decades.* It had only been three weeks since Malcolm arrived at the O'Donnell house, though.

Jennifer pulled away from Malcolm and sniffled as she examined his face, running her eyes over every scratch and bruise.

She caressed his hair and, in a shaky voice, she said, "I'm sorry, Malcolm. I've been looking for you for days, I've been trying to get you out of that house, but I couldn't do it. I took too long." She looked down at her son's battered abdomen and broken leg. She said, "Look at what they did to you because... because of me, because I was scared. I should have never brought you to him. I'm so sorry."

Malcolm responded, "It's okay, mom. I forgive you. I don't care about any of that anyway. It's over now and... and I'm just happy to see you."

"I'm happy to see you, too, baby. I missed you so much."

Jennifer hugged him again, pulling his face close to her chest while nuzzling his hair. Malcolm, who wasn't very affectionate around his mother, did not resist her. He felt safe and comfortable in her arms, like a newborn baby. He thought about his nightmarish experience at the house and he thought about the actions that led him there.

He said, "Mom, I'm sorry."

Her brow raised, Jennifer pulled away from her son and asked, "For what, kiddo?"

"You brought me here, but that was because of me. I decided to break the rules at home, and I did it over and over again. You had to do something and I understand that. This is my fault and I'm sorry."

"No. No, Malcolm, you have nothing to be sorry about. You broke the rules, but that doesn't mean you deserved... *this*. I wasn't a good mother and I tried to take a shortcut. I wanted your grandfather to help you grow because I felt like I wasn't good enough. That's the truth."

"You are a good mother. You–You're a great mom. You're the best mom."

He took a moment to swallow the lump in his throat. He looked around the room, memories running rampant in his mind—*flashbacks.*

Avoiding eye contact, he said, "I've seen real bad parents. Ronald and Barbara... I don't know what they were like when you were younger, but they were evil in that house. Pure evil. You know, I can't imagine what you went through growing up with them when you were a kid. I was only with them for a few weeks, you were there for years. It was a nightmare... a fucking nightmare."

Jennifer frowned upon spotting the agony in his eyes—the mental suffering. She gently rubbed his hands and caressed his face. They spent an hour exchanging apologies, discussing Malcolm's experience at the house, and talking about the future—a bright future.

"Hey," Claire said from the doorway.

Malcolm and Jennifer looked over at her, surprised by her soft voice. Jennifer met her at the police station before she visited the hospital, so they were acquainted. Malcolm smiled, looked away, and scrubbed the dried tears from his cheeks.

Claire approached the bed and said, "You look better, Malcolm. How are you feeling?"

"I–I'm okay. I'm, um... I'm trapped on this bed, but it's a lot better than that bunker."

"Yeah, I can tell. You're safe here. I'm happy for you."

Jennifer rubbed Malcolm's shoulder and smirked. She said, "You two make a cute couple."

Malcolm lowered his head and said, "Mom, this is Claire—Claire Olson. She's my, um... She's my–"

"I'm his girlfriend," Claire declared, blushing.

"Yeah, she's my girlfriend."

The group smiled and laughed. The exuberant

mood in the room swiftly vanished, though, replaced with a grim silence. There was a lot on Claire's mind. *Murderer*—that word kept echoing through her head. She set off the chain of events that led to so much violence. Taking a life wasn't as easy as it looked in the movies. She was disturbed by her tardiness, too.

Claire said, "Malcolm, I'm sorry for coming so late."

"It's not late. My mom just got here an hour ago. It's still–"

"I meant, going to that house so late. I tried my best to help, but I took way too long. I... I messed up."

"You saved me, Claire. If you didn't come when you did, I would have been eaten alive by rats. You pulled me out of hell and gave me a chance to live again. I'll never forget that. I owe you more than a fancy dinner."

Claire smiled through her tears. She responded, "I'm glad you didn't forget that, but I think a hospital dinner would be better than a 'fancy' dinner."

"Yeah, that sounds good, too."

Tap, tap, tap—the knocking emerged from the door. Detective Anthony Howard stood in the doorway, a thin smile on his face. He wore a long tweed coat, a white button-up shirt with a black tie, black trousers, and matching dress shoes. His brown eyes looked stern, but he gave off a benign aura.

Howard stepped into the room and said, "I hope I'm not interrupting anything. My name is Anthony Howard and I'm with the police department. I was hoping to have a word with you."

Jennifer nodded and said, "Okay, sure."

"Should I leave?" Claire asked.

Howard asked, "You're Claire Olson, correct?" Claire nodded. Howard said, "You can stick around. I'm not going to question any of you in this room. I just want to make some things clear."

The detective approached the foot of the bed. He looked down at Malcolm, saddened by his severe injuries. He had already seen the teenager, he knew all about the case, but he was still caught off guard.

He said, "We understand that you were abused by your grandparents, Ronald and Barbara O'Donnell. We will interview you about that when you're feeling better. It's going to be difficult to relive the past, but we need your story in order to properly close this case. I hope you'll cooperate."

Malcolm clenched his jaw and took a deep breath, then he nodded. Images of violence flashed in his mind. Although painful, he knew the memories were important.

Howard continued, "Good. Most importantly, I want to personally inform you that there is an ongoing internal investigation regarding your calls, yours and Claire's. There were some issues, the calls may have been mishandled, but we'll get to the bottom of it. This will never happen again. You have my word on that."

The detective's words were genuine, but Malcolm didn't have anything to say to him. He remained quiet and he kept nodding.

Howard said, "I'll be back to talk to you later, Malcolm. Get better, kid." He glanced over at Jennifer and said, "Ms. Hernandez, do you mind joining me? I'd like to have a word with you in a more private setting."

"Sure, sure," Jennifer responded, a pinch of concern in her voice. She kissed Malcolm's forehead and said, "I'll come see you as soon as I'm done with this. I love you, kiddo."

As they approached the door, Malcolm said, "Wait." They stopped and looked back at him. Malcolm said, "Please don't punish my mom for any of this. She's not responsible, she didn't ask them to do this to me. If anything, you should only punish Ronald and Barbara, but they... they're dead."

Howard said, "We'll see what happens. Your mother seems like an innocent person, though. As for your grandparents, your grandmother passed away in the fire, but your grandfather is still alive. I'll make sure he's locked up for the rest of his life. Get some rest, kid. I'll talk to you soon."

Malcolm was shocked by the revelation. He stared blankly at the doorway, even after Jennifer and Howard exited the room. *The old man is still alive,* he thought, *he can lie his way out of this, he can still win.* He clenched his fists and shook his head. The gesture said: *no, fuck that.* He lifted his broken leg, which was wrapped in a cast, from the elevation pillow.

Eyes wide with concern, Claire asked, "What are you doing?"

"Do me a favor, Claire. If that old man is still alive, I want you to find him. If he's in this hospital, tell me his room number."

"Wha–What? Why?"

"Just do it."

"Why, Malcolm?"

"Because this isn't over until he's dead, okay? It's not over yet, damn it," Malcolm snapped. Claire took a step back, startled. Malcolm sighed, then he said, "Please, just find him for me. If you don't, I'll have to find him myself. One way or another, I have to do this."

Claire saw a mixture of sorrow and determination in Malcolm's eyes. If she didn't help him, she knew he would limp from room-to-room until he found Ronald, inevitably harming himself and others. She opened her mouth to speak, but she couldn't say a word. So, she nodded in agreement and exited the room.

While Claire searched for Ronald's room, Malcolm prepared himself for the final confrontation. He pulled the IV out of his arm, causing a jet of blood to squirt out of his arm, then he staggered off the bed. While searching for a weapon in his room, he noticed the moonlight coming through the windows—it was late.

"I have to work fast," Malcolm whispered.

To his dismay, he couldn't find any suitable weapons in the room. *The bed sheets? The food tray? The IV tube?*–he thought.

Claire returned after ten minutes, constantly glancing over her shoulder as if she were being followed. She leaned closer to Malcolm, her lips sucked into her mouth. Her doubt was obvious.

She whispered, "Are you sure about this, Malcolm? I mean, are you really sure?"

"I'm positive? Where is he? Huh? Is he in this hospital?"

"He's in this hospital, on this floor, but I don't

know if–"

"Which room?"

Claire sighed, then she said, "He's in 232. Take a left, then take a right before you get to the elevators. It's the last door on the left in that hall." She grabbed Malcolm's hand and said, "You don't have to do this. He's not worth it. Let the system take care of him."

"The system couldn't take care of me because of him. My grandma is dead and he deserves to burn in hell with her. That's the way it is."

Tears streamed across Claire's rosy cheeks as she looked up at the ceiling. She was conflicted by thoughts of love and shame. She could tell a nurse or a cop about Malcolm's plan, but she couldn't throw him under the bus.

Malcolm said, "Go home. I don't want you to get in trouble."

Claire loudly swallowed the lump in her throat, then she said, "I want to see you again, but not in a jail cell. Don't do something you'll regret."

"I won't regret a thing."

"I hope you're right about that."

The couple shared a kiss. Claire exited the room and departed from the hospital.

Malcolm waited for three minutes, then he peeked into the corridor—the coast was clear. The cameras would surely catch him, but that was a problem for another day. He limped down the hall, dragging his broken leg behind him. *Go left until you reach the elevators,* he thought.

At the elevators, he took a right and whispered, "Then go right."

He limped past the rooms, ignoring the

slumbering patients and wandering nurses. Fortunately for him, they ignored him, too.

He whispered, "The last door on the left."

He stood in the doorway and stared into the dark room. The machines beside the bed *beeped* and *clicked.* The oxygen concentrator emitted a *hissing* sound.

Ronald lay in bed, an oxygen mask covering his mouth and nose. His wounds had been treated, bullets removed from his body and given to the police. He needed help breathing, but he looked like he would survive. He could not, however, fight against his grandson. He was bedridden, he was vulnerable.

Malcolm approached the bed, examining every inch of his grandfather's body. He cycled through his options: unplug everything, smother him with a pillow, strangle him with his bare hands, beat him to death. There were so many ways to kill a man, even in a safe, secure hospital room. He grabbed an empty flower vase from the bedside table. Disregarding the noise, he smashed the vase on the table.

The vase *exploded* into a dozen shards, as loud as the sound of a chandelier falling in an empty room.

Ronald awoke, his eyelids flickering. Without turning his head, he looked to his right. Through his blurred vision, he spotted a figure standing in front of the light that entered the room through the doorway. The figure resembled a blot of ink on white paper—round, black, distorted, and surrounded by white light.

He couldn't identify the person because of his

blurred vision. The darkness in the room didn't help, either. However, he knew his enemy well. The battle wasn't over.

A large shard of glass in his right hand, Malcolm glared at Ronald and said, "You fucking bastard, you almost killed me. For what? Huh? *For what?* To teach me a lesson? To make me into a man? To... To kill my 'Aztec' genes? No, that was all bullshit. You did it because you're a monster, and you've always been a monster. The people out there think you're some sort of war hero, but I'm going to tell them the truth. I'm going to tell my story, I'm going to show them those pictures from the attic. Your name, your legacy... It's going to be hated around the world."

Ronald didn't respond, but he heard every word. His eyes, wide and protuberant, dilated with fear. Beads of sweat, cold and plentiful, glistened on his brow. He didn't fear death—death came for everyone. He only feared the tainting of his good name.

Malcolm thrust the shard into Ronald's limp forearm. The shard traveled across his vein until it stopped at his wrist. Then he stabbed his forearm again and repeated the process. He cut his forearm vertically five times with the shard. His right arm was drenched in blood—blood that looked black in the dark room.

Ronald looked down at his sliced arm as tears welled in his eyes. The *beep* of the heart monitor accelerated.

Malcolm approached the other side of the bed. He turned off the heart monitor, hoping to buy himself some time. Instead of cutting his left wrist vertically, he cut his wrist horizontally. He sawed into his wrist until he scraped at his bone with the shard. He saw red, white, and yellow in the deep gash. His hand was barely attached to his wrist. It looked as if it would fall off at any moment.

The shard even cut into Malcolm's fingers, but the pain didn't bother him. He had been through far worse. He placed the shard in Ronald's trembling hand.

He leaned closer to Ronald's face, looked him in the eye, and said, "I'm going to be a better man than you. I'm going to take care of my mom. I'm going to love Claire. And, when I'm older, I'm going to treat my children and grandchildren right. If you taught me anything in that bunker, it's that... that I'm *not* like you. I'm a human, not a monster. I'll see you in hell, old man."

Ronald opened his mouth behind the mask, but he couldn't say a word. He blinked slowly—once, twice, thrice. He didn't open his eyes after the third blink. He died a slow, painful death.

Malcolm turned towards the door, but he quickly stopped himself. A police officer stood in the doorway. He recognized the man—Keith Griffin, the cop who first visited the O'Donnell house. Griffin witnessed most of the crime. He watched as Malcolm sliced Ronald's left wrist and he listened to the teenager's passionate speech. He was rendered speechless by the situation.

Malcolm stood in silence, blood dripping from his fingertips. He was ready to accept the consequences of his actions.

A hint of uncertainty in his voice, Griffin

stuttered, "G–Get out. G–Go. Get out of here, kid." Malcolm furrowed his brow and cocked his head back, baffled. The cop repeated, "*Get out.*"

Malcolm nodded slowly. He wrapped his gown around his bleeding hand, then he squeezed past the officer and limped into the hall. He took one final glance at the officer, confused by his decision, then he returned to his bed. He lay in bed, curled in the fetal position. He thought about Griffin's motives. *He let me go because he felt guilty,* he thought, *he did it because he didn't stop this when he had the chance.*

He didn't know if Griffin could keep him out of trouble, but he appreciated the effort. He closed his eyes and counted sheep, but to no avail. Sleep was out of the question. Guilt, anger, and fear clung to his mind. He was haunted by his horrific experience at his grandfather's house—an experience he would *never* forget.

Join the mailing list!

Did you enjoy your visit to the O'Donnell house? Want to read more dark, disturbing, and provocative horror books? If so, you should join my mailing list. I publish an extreme horror book nearly every month —sometimes I even publish two in a single month! By signing up for my mailing list, you'll receive an email whenever I release a new book and you'll be the first to know about any of my book sales. You won't miss a thing. Best of all, the process requires very little effort and it's completely *free.*

By signing up, you'll only receive 1-2 emails per month. If I'm having a very big sale or if I'm releasing multiple books, you might receive three emails a month, but that's usually not necessary. You won't get any spam, either. Click here to sign-up: http://eepurl.com/bNl1CP

Dear Reader,

Hey! Thanks for reading *Grandfather's House*. Like most of my work, this was a very violent novel. It's not the most brutal book I've ever written, but I think some scenes pushed the boundaries of horror. Also, like my other novels, there were plenty of **warnings** plastered on this book—on the back of the paperback, in the front matter, and on the product page. Yet, I'm sure someone, somewhere, was offended by the contents of this book. It happens all the time. Regardless, if you were offended, if you stumbled upon this book by mistake or if you just decided to ignore the warnings, I want to apologize. I'm not some edgy teenager who writes to offend people. I write books like these to horrify.

This book wasn't inspired by anything in particular. I suppose it was inspired by human nature—the dark side of the human mind. I wrote a book about abuse before: *The Abuse of Ashley Collins.* It was a popular book by indie standards and, although it dealt with a dark subject, I enjoyed writing it. In a sense, I wanted to recreate that book with *Grandfather's House.* This time around, however, I wanted to focus on character, suspense, and even drama, instead of all-out violence. I hoped to create a more realistic depiction of the cycle of abuse. Yes, there are some outlandish scenes in this novel, but it's not completely out of the ordinary, especially if you've been paying attention to the news in recent years.

People are unpredictable.

Of course, this book was inspired by others like it as well. I had just finished reading *The Girl Next Door* by Jack Ketchum again before I started writing this one. As a matter of fact, I've been reading a lot of Jack Ketchum lately, so his work has once again been inspiring some of mine. (Note: I wrote this letter *before* Dallas Mayr/Jack Ketchum's unfortunate passing on January 24th, 2018. Rest in peace.) I watched the *Flowers in the Attic* (1987) for the first time before delving into this project, too, so I suppose that also lent some inspiration. I haven't read the book, though. Is it any good? Do you recommend it? There isn't a lot of fiction on the subject. I suppose that's a good thing for some people. It's definitely not a comfortable subject, but that's part of the horror.

If you enjoyed this book, it would help a lot if you left a review on Amazon.com. Your reviews may not seem like much, but they are extremely helpful. Your reviews help me improve on my writing, it helps me pick my next project, and it helps other readers find this book. Good or bad, your reviews lead to more books—better books. Of course, the exposure also helps me make a living. If you need help, here are some questions you can answer to get you started. Did you enjoy the story? Did you connect to the characters? Did the story horrify you? Was this a provocative experience? Did this book leave an impression? Would you like to read more books like this? Answering questions like these will help me understand you. Feel free to leave your own comments, too, or send me an email!

You can show more support by sharing this book. Post a link to this book on Facebook or Twitter, share the awesome cover on Instagram or Snapchat, write a post about it on your blog, buy a paperback for yourself or ship one out to a friend, buy a Kindle copy for a distant friend/relative, or share this novel with your book club. By the way, if you buy a paperback of any of my books, you get a *free* Kindle version. That's an awesome deal, right? Sharing books, or word-of-mouth, really helps your favorite authors—or your not-so-favorite authors. It's a great way to make new friends, too.

In terms of my personal life, I've been doing well these days. I'm not super wealthy, I'm actually not wealthy at all now that I think of it, but I am kinda happy... I think? You know how it is. I still have to thank you, though. Every month, I get closer and closer to becoming a fully independent, full-time author, and it's all thanks to you. Whether you purchase the Kindle versions, buy the paperbacks, or read my books through Kindle Unlimited, your support has been tremendous. I never imagined I would get this far doing this. Hopefully, with the extra money I make from writing, I'll be able to experience more of life. In turn, I'll be able to write more *unique* books. That's the goal, at least. And again, even if this is the first book of mine that you've read, thank you very much.

Finally, if you're a horror fan, feel free to visit my Amazon's Author page. I've published nearly two dozen horror novels, a few sci-fi/fantasy books, and some anthologies. Want to read a violent story of revenge and human horror? Check out *Sympathy for the Widow*. Next month, which is April 2018, I'll be releasing *Party Games*. It's a book about a group of friends who are held hostage in a cabin in the woods by a group of delinquent sadists. If you're new to my work, please feel free to check out some of my older novels, too. Some of them are actually pretty good according to reviewers. If you've read them all already, you're an awesome person. You know this already, too: I release a new book every month, so another one will be out soon. Once again, thank you for reading. Your readership keeps me going through the darkest times!

Until our next venture into the dark and disturbing,
Jon Athan

P.S. If you have questions (or insults), you can contact me through my business email: *info@jon-athan.com*. I love hearing from readers, even if it's just a short comment. You can also contact me via Twitter @Jonny_Athan, or my Facebook page. Thanks again!